RYAN'S RETURN

After the break-up of her marriage Liv Denison had made a nice and satisfactory life for herself—alone. The last thing she wanted was her husband Ryan coming back to spoil it. He had hurt her before and she was determined he wasn't going to do it again. But somewhere deep inside her a tiny ember had continued to glow . . .

RYAN'S RETURN

BY

LYNSEY STEVENS

MILLS & BOON LIMITED
15–16 BROOK'S MEWS
LONDON W1A 1DR

First published 1981
Australian copyright 1981
Philippine copyright 1981
This edition 1981

© Lynsey Stevens 1981

ISBN 0 263 73536 2

Set in Monophoto Baskerville 11 on 12 pt.

Made and printed in Great Britain by
Richard Clay (The Chaucer Press) Ltd,
Bungay, Suffolk

CHAPTER ONE

FLEXING her aching muscles, Liv sat back and smiled with satisfaction at the delicately painted miniature china vase she had completed at last. She added her signature to the bottom with a final flourish: Liv Denison. Now it was ready to be fired and then added to the box of various other pieces of china she had painted which had such a ready market at the Gift Inn at Airlie Beach. Although she preferred her oil painting she knew a certain self-fulfilment when she finished each tiny piece of china, perfect in its miniaturisation.

Her success with her painting both in oils and on china could still move Liv to incredulity, even after five years. The whole thing began while she was doing a little part-time work minding a local souvenir shop. The owner had been impressed with a painting she had taken along to the shop to be framed and had asked to display two of Liv's seascapes. These had sold almost immediately and since then Liv had managed to make a comfortable living from the sale of her canvases and, lately, her pieces of hand-painted china, doing especially well in the tourist season.

Now she had one small room in her three-bedroom bungalow set aside as her studio and all the paraphernalia associated with what began as a hobby was stacked about her. On one easel rested a completed seascape while another held a canvas in its early stages, and stacked neatly about the floor were other canvases ready for painting or framing. Tubes of oil paints and a number of palettes were lying on a nearby table.

Liv cleaned her brushes and replaced them on the shelf and, glancing at her wristwatch, hurried into the bathroom for a quick shower. Twenty minutes later she was in the kitchen, an apron tied over her clean pale blue and white dress. The twins would be home in less than half an hour and Joel could arrive any time. She set the three plates of chicken and salad on the table and covered them with individual pieces of clear plastic food wrap before stowing them carefully in the refrigerator.

'Hey, Liv! Your babysitter has arrived,' a cheerful voice hailed her from the open front door as she was washing her hands.

'Come on in, Joel. I'm in the kitchen,' she called, smiling as her brother-in-law came down the hallway with his easy strides. 'Feel strong enough to last out the evening with the twins?'

'I'm looking forward to it. You know they're never any trouble,' he grinned.

At twenty-nine Joel Denison was one of the most eligible bachelors in the district, and it always amazed Liv that he hadn't married and had a family of his own. He was wonderful with the twins and she knew he was one of the nicest, kindest men you could meet anywhere.

'As a matter of fact I'd have taken on a whole classroom full of seven-year-olds tonight. Anything to get out of the house!' he told her.

'Oh! What's the trouble?' Liv handed him a cup of

tea and they sat companionably down at the small kitchen table.

'D.J. What else?' Joel pulled a rueful face as he sipped his tea. 'You know, that man can run rings around me mentally and I can give him over thirty years. How do you suppose he ever ended up with a son like me?'

'He was just lucky, I guess,' Liv's blue eyes shone as she dimpled teasingly. 'Maybe you were mixed up in the hospital.'

'That's a possibility,' Joel laughed with her.

'Anyway, what's D.J. been up to this time?' She raised a fine eyebrow, knowing from past personal experience how strongminded her father-in-law could be.

'It's not what D.J.'s been up to this time but what old Mrs Craven has done.'

'Old Mrs Craven? Of Craven Island . . .?' Liv looked incredulously at Joel as the light dawned. 'You don't mean she's sold out after all this time?'

'Oh yes, I do! Could be the start of World War Three.'

'But she swore she never would sell Craven Island. It's been in her family for three generations and she's always refused all offers made for any of her property in the past.'

'Well, apparently now she's changed her mind. And not only has she sold the island,' Joel set his cup down on his saucer, 'but also that block of land she has up on the hill overlooking the harbour. Must have gone as a package deal.'

'Good grief! No wonder D.J.'s livid.' Liv could imagine her father-in-law's anger. It was common knowledge that D. J. Denison had wanted both properties for years, as long as Liv could remember anyway, and the old lady had repeatedly refused to sell to him, or to anyone else, for that matter.

'Do you know who bought them?'

'That's the point, Liv. Nobody seems to know. D.J. has turned every stone trying to find out, but even he's drawn a blank. Personally, I think it would be safe to say it's no one local.' Joel shrugged his shoulders. 'Who could come up with the kind of cash Mrs Craven would have been asking? D.J.'s got it in his head that it's a syndicate and that eventually the state government will change its policy and we'll end up with a casino or some such, either up on the hill or over on the island.'

'Oh, Joel, no! They wouldn't.'

'Who can say? I really couldn't see Mrs Craven selling on those terms, but you know how D.J. feels about that kind of thing. At least his ideas on an island resort were to keep the island as near to natural as possible.'

'But surely someone must know something about the sale? I mean, there have to be solicitors involved with the legal side of the transaction, and that means Mr Willis. He handles all Mrs Craven's affairs, doesn't he?'

'If old Willis is involved he's playing it very close to the chest. Knowing he was Mrs Craven's solicitor D.J. went there first.' Joel laughed. 'A little word like "confidential" doesn't mean much to D.J.! Anyway, he was none the wiser after speaking to the solicitor. Crikey, he was mad! I thought he was going to have a stroke. He tackled Mrs Craven on the phone as well and you could hear him yelling from one end of the house to the other.' Joel shook his head. 'I haven't seen him so mad since . . .' He stopped and flushed slightly. 'Well, in ages,' he finished quickly.

An uncomfortable silence fell over them for a few moments as Joel's unspoken words hung tensely between them. Neither looked at the other, although they were both thinking the same thing. Since that time with you and Ryan.

'When are the twins due home?' Joel changed the subject and the moment slowly passed.

Liv glanced at the kitchen clock. 'Should be here any time now. Maria Costello collected them from school and they've been playing with Dino and little Sophy for the afternoon. She said she'd drop them home around five o'clock.'

Joel nodded. 'With a bit of luck they'll be so tired from running around all afternoon that we'll be able to settle for a nice peaceful unstrenuous game of snakes and ladders or something. Last time I babysat they wore me out playing soccer until I almost expired. Luckily for me darkness fell, saved me by the skin of my teeth. Shows how out of condition I am,' he grinned.

'You'll have to put your foot down with a firm hand,' Liv laughed. 'You're far too soft with them, Joel.'

'Oh, well. Who needs an ogre for an uncle anyway? They're great kids, Liv.'

'I know they are,' she chuckled, 'but I guess that sounds very prejudiced coming from their mother. Ah, speak of my little devils, that sounds like them now.'

Liv walked along the hall to the door in time to wave to Maria Costello before the twins bounded up the steps and into her arms.

'Hi, Mum! What's for dinner?' Luke tossed his

school bag on to the small table inside the door. 'I'm famished!'

'Is Uncle Joe here yet?' Melly put her own school bag on the table with less vigour.

'Mmm, he's in the kitchen. Go and talk to him while I finish getting dressed. And no biscuits, Luke, you'll spoil your dinner,' she called after her son as he raced into the kitchen, followed more slowly by his sister.

Liv applied a little light make-up to her face, a dusting of blue eye-shadow to her eyelids, a touch of mascara to the tips of her eyelashes, finishing with some pale pink gloss on her lips. Undoing the clasp holding back her long fair hair, she brushed it until it was tidy. She was about to pull it back again into the more severe style she usually wore when, on impulse, she let it fall back about her face. Turning slightly, she could see in the mirror that it almost reached her waist at the back and the artificial light over her dressing table highlighted its healthy sheen, giving it the appearance of liquid silk. It was only in the past couple of years that she had allowed her hair to grow down past her shoulders, always preferring to have it short and manageable. Impatiently she clasped it back and secured it neatly. She was being unusually fanciful tonight.

Her eyes moved over her reflection. Large blue eyes fringed by long lashes set in a reasonably attractive face looked back at her from the mirror. No great beauty, she told herself, but not bad for someone who was fast approaching her twenty-fifth birthday. She grinned, allowing her gaze to fall downwards over her figure, pursing her lips ruefully. Definitely unfashionable, she thought, surveying her full breasts, narrow waist and rounded hips. At five foot six inches she could not be called short and in an era of slender petiteness she often felt gargantuan.

She could hear laughter from the kitchen, Joel's teasing banter, Luke's unrestrained chortle, Melly's amused giggle. Whenever Joel was around there seemed to be laughter. Had she had a brother he couldn't have meant more to her than Joel did. She didn't know how she would have managed without him over the years. He had always been there when she needed him, even in the beginning of it all, when she knew she had hurt and disappointed him. And everyone else whose life had touched upon hers and Ryan's.

Ryan. She closed her eyes to shut out the name. What had brought him to her mind this evening? She hadn't thought about him in ages, and now . . . She blinked and turned purposefully towards the door. And she wasn't going to think about him now, she told herself forcefully. Martin would be arriving any minute. They were going out to dinner and then on to a Parents and Teachers Association meeting at the school the twins attended.

'Your dinner's prepared and in the fridge, Joel,' she said, joining them in the kitchen. 'Sure you don't mind bathing the twins as well?' she frowned.

'Of course not. I've brought my wet suit along especially for the occasion,' he winked at the twins, causing more laughter. 'Stop fussing, Liv. Just go out and have a great time. You don't get out enough as it is.'

'We'll be very good, Mummy,' said Melly solemnly, wrapping her arms about Liv's waist. 'Mmm, you smell delicious.'

Liv brushed the dark hair back from her daughter's

forehead and looking down into her deep blue eyes she felt a pang that Melly could look so much like her father and yet have a nature that was so soft and gentle. Ryan had been one hundred per cent steel.

'I'll even behave,' said Luke, tapping his chest with his thumb and widening his blue eyes in innocence. Luke was as fair as his sister was dark, taking his colouring from Liv, and was as outgoing as Melly was shy and retiring. They were as different as chalk and cheese, and her heart contracted painfully with love for them. For the hundredth time she wondered how something as beautiful as her children could have resulted from something so cheap and sordid.

'There's your escort,' Joel nodded towards the door as the bell pealed. 'Right on the dot. I just wish you were off somewhere more exciting than dinner and a P.T.A. meeting. I'll have to talk to Martin Wilson.'

'Yes—well, I won't be late, Joel.' Liv gave herself a mental shake to get herself going.

'Liv, stay out till dawn if you want to, only have a good time. Dr Joel Denison absolutely insists.' He gave her a gentle push towards the door with a sigh of exasperation. 'If you don't answer the door bell soon you'll have to stay and eat with us, and that's a threat,' he teased.

Before she knew it Liv was sitting beside Martin in his early model Holden, heading towards Airlie Beach.

'I hope you're going to enjoy the meal, Olivia. I'm afraid I haven't tried this particular restaurant before this evening.' Martin Wilson glanced sideways at Liv's pale face.

'I'm sure I shall, Martin. I've only heard good reports about the place.' She forced herself to respond cheerfully and was relieved when she saw the concern vanish from his face. An inquisition by Martin was the last thing she needed tonight.

Martin was a teacher at the school the twins attended and she had met him at a P.T.A. meeting last year when he had been transferred to the school. Their friendship had begun slowly and neither of them felt the need to rush into any binding relationship, least of all herself. She wasn't sure she wanted a relationship with anyone ever again.

The fact that Martin had suggested this dinner had Liv just slightly perplexed. He didn't make a habit of taking her out, preferring to meet her at functions they both attended, and this had suited Liv quite well. No, she mused, Martin didn't rush into anything. He plotted his life with thought and clinical calculations and at thirty his fair sandy hair was thinning noticeably and although he wasn't handsome his air of self-confidence and sober disposition made him adequate if unexciting company.

They spent an enjoyable hour and a half over dinner and a little longer at their meeting at the primary school before heading back around the bays. For some reason Liv had felt slightly out of sorts all evening, ill at ease, and at times it was all she could do to force herself to concentrate on what Martin was saying. However, he loved to talk and didn't seem to have noticed anything amiss. In fact, at this moment he was looking a trifle smug after coming out on top in a debate with one of the harridans on the committee.

Watching his hands as he drove the car sedately around the bay adhering religiously to the speed limit, Liv experienced a pang of irritation and found her mind flashing vividly back to another night she had travelled this very road clinging half in terror and half in exhilaration to the soft leather seat of an E-type Jaguar as a pair of strong hands threw the car around the bends, breaking all rules and regulations, defying gravity, white teeth flashing in a tanned face.

That face rose before her, so real in each detail that she almost gasped, and her hands clutched together in her lap. The firm square jaw with the hint of a cleft in the chin. The curving lips with their promised sensuality. The straight aristocratic nose. The furrow in each cheek when he laughed. And the most incredibly dark blue eyes fringed by long dark lashes. Eyes so deep she used to feel herself lost in their compelling depths. His hair had always hung down over his collar, one unruly dark lock falling over his forehead, giving him an air of piratic attractiveness.

Martin's mentioning of Luke's name brought her back to the present with a start.

'I'm sorry, Martin. What were you saying?'

'Just that I'd heard Luke had been in trouble again,' Martin repeated.

'Luke? He didn't say anything,' Liv frowned. 'What did he do?'

'I'm not sure of the whole story. Something to do with a fight involving young Costello.'

'Oh, that!' Liv sighed with relief. 'I know all about that. Actually Luke tried to stop the fight. The other boy was a lot older than Dino Costello.'

'You know, Olivia, a boy needs a firm hand, a father to guide him.'

'Don't you think I know that, Martin.' Liv felt her irritation rise again. 'I love my children and I'm trying to bring them up the best way I know how.'

'I'm sorry, Olivia, I didn't mean to sound as though I was being critical. I appreciate the problems you have to face.' Martin paused for a few moments. 'Have you ever thought about getting a divorce?'

'A divorce?' Liv mouthed the word as though it was unfamiliar to her. 'No,' she said softly and then a little louder, 'No, I haven't, Martin.'

'What about your husband? Has he ever approached you to dissolve your marriage?'

'No.' For an inexplicable reason a cold hand seemed to have clutched about her heart. 'We don't correspond,' she said flatly.

'Not ever?'

'No.' Silence fell as they turned along the beach front towards Liv's bungalow. They passed a car parked by the roadside and Liv caught the glow of a cigarette end without consciously noticing it, passing it off as a courting couple. Once she'd parked along the beach here with Ryan . . .

'I've never asked before, but what happened between you and your husband? You weren't together long, were you?'

Liv almost welcomed Martin's interruption of her thoughts. The past seemed to be playing on her mind tonight and she had a feeling that that past was still as painful as it had ever been. Looking down at her lap, she was distantly surprised to see that her hands were still clutched together, the knuckles white, and she forced herself to relax them.

How could she answer Martin's question? What could she say? Nothing. Nothing had happened between Ryan and herself because nothing ever really started, except for one brief coming together that neither of them could . . . Nothing! Simply nothing! She could feel hysterical laughter stir deep within her.

Martin sighed. 'You don't have to talk about it if it upsets you, but I thought we were friends—good friends.' He pulled the Holden to a halt behind Joel's car in front of her bungalow and switched off the ignition, turning towards her and taking her hands in his. 'Olivia, before we go in, I've been meaning to discuss this with you for some time. I feel I'm now settled in my career and I have a steady income and a little put by. I need a wife, Olivia, and I think you and I could make a very good life together.'

Liv felt panic rise in her throat. She wasn't ready for this kind of involvement with Martin, with anyone. 'Martin, please, I've never thought along those lines—I mean, I . . .'

'I know I've not picked the best time to discuss such a serious subject with you and I don't want to pressure you, but I'd like you to think it over. That's all I ask—just think it over.' He lifted her hand to his lips for a moment. 'Will you do that?'

'All right, Martin.' Anything to bring this evening to an end. She had all but cringed away, revolted by the touch of his lips on her hand. What could be wrong with her? Everything was crowding in on her, building up, stretching her nerves to tautness until she had a desire to run, to get away from it all, escape back to a world where she had no decisions to make, where she didn't have to think about it.

'Good.' Martin smiled, happily unaware of the turmoil inside her. He climbed out of the car and walked around to open her door for her, his hand resting on her elbow as they walked up the path.

The porch light glowed and Joel opened the door before Liv could reach for her key. Her brother-in-law's smiling face brought with it a little calmness, righted the swaying topsy-turviness of the chaos within her.

'Hi! Had a good evening? You're just in time for coffee,' Joel smiled easily.

'Yes, we've had a most enjoyable evening, thank you,' replied Martin with stiff formality.

'Twins asleep? I hope they weren't too much trouble?' Liv followed Joel thankfully down the hallway, tossing her light jacket on a chair back while Joel collected two extra coffee mugs.

'They were fine and they're sleeping like angels. Melly was just about asleep over her dinner.' Joel drained his coffee cup. 'Well, I'll call it a night. I suspect I'm going to have a full day tomorrow, what with one thing and another.' He raised a meaningful eyebrow at Liv. 'Don't forget dinner at the house tomorrow night. D.J. told me to remind you. I'll pick you all up at seven o'clock as usual—okay?'

'That will be fine, Joel. I'll see you then.' Liv had to stop herself from imploring him to stay. She didn't want to spend any more time alone with Martin tonight, and if that was being cowardly, she didn't care.

'Don't get up, Liv. I'll see myself out.' Joel walked quickly down the hallway. 'I'll see you, Martin.'

'Does Denison watch the children for you very often?' Martin asked, a hint of criticism in his tone.

'Yes. Not that I need a babysitter very often, but Joel usually comes over if I don't leave the twins with Mick and Maria Costello,' Liv murmured evenly. 'Why?'

'Oh, nothing.' Martin turned his coffee mug a

couple of times, watching the dark liquid. 'I just thought you would have been loath to have anything to do with the Denisons after you and your husband broke up.'

'None of it had anything to do with Joel, Martin,' Liv said sharply.

'I'm not saying that it did.' Martin held up his hand. 'Of course, you know best. He seems a nice enough fellow.'

'He is, very nice. If there were more Joel Denisons in the world it would be a better place.'

'I suppose old Mr Denison likes to see his grand-children now and then.' When Liv made no comment Martin finished his coffee. 'Yes, well, it is getting late. I must be getting home myself. Saturday is my house-hold chores day,' he smiled, getting to his feet.

Out on the porch he turned and pulled her into his arms with uncharacteristic firmness, holding her lightly against him. 'Thank you for this evening, Olivia.'

'Thank you for taking me, Martin.' Her words sounded stilted, expressionless, and she willed her tense body to relax, without very much success. She shivered slightly, feeling an uncanny eeriness, as though an unseen eye was watching.

Martin released her immediately. 'You're cold. The breeze can be quite fresh coming straight off the water. You don't want to catch a chill.'

Liv rubbed her arms. 'Yes, it is rather cool. I'd better go in.'

Martin leant down and she turned her face slightly so that his kiss fell on her cheek. 'I'll say goodnight, then. I'll ring you some time next week if I don't see you at school first. You will think over what I've said, won't you?'

She stood watching the tail-lights of Martin's car disappear along the bay road. The light-coloured car they had passed earlier was still parked by the road, momentarily illuminated in Martin's headlights. Liv shivered again and walked inside, locking the door after her.

She checked on Luke, pulling the sheets he had cast aside back over his spreadeagled body. He sighed deeply as she turned him into a more comfortable position. Liv and Melly shared the other bedroom and Liv quietly undressed and pulled her short cotton nightdress over her head. Undoing her hair, she sat in the semi-darkness brushing it absently, trying to still her racing mind.

It was no good, of course. She'd never sleep at the moment. So she returned to the kitchen, pulling the door closed on her soundly sleeping daughter. The disquietened mood that had come upon her before she went out still sat heavily upon her and she knew sleep was miles away.

The whole crux of the matter seemed to be that memories from the past kept sweeping over her. After eight years she thought it had all been relegated nicely into the background, something that had occurred, that she had weathered and set behind her. Her hands stilled as she washed the used coffee cups. What had brought thoughts of Ryan back to her tonight?

It wasn't as though she allowed herself to think about him. In fact, she thought she had brainwashed herself over the years into completely wiping him from her mind. She smiled cynically to herself. So much for that. Her recollections tonight proved he was as real as he had ever been.

The kitchen light lit the outside patio through the open door with a soft mellow glow and Liv strolled out into the night, smiling as the breeze lifted her hair, cooling her body through the thinness of her nightdress. She rested her elbows on the railings and took a deep breath of the fresh salty air.

The bungalow sat some hundred feet from the white sand of the beach and the incoming tide rippled and lapped soothingly on the sand, twinkling in the moonlight. The moonlit sky was a mass of stars and the only signs of any other habitation were the few lights of distant houses near the wharf around to the left of the bay. The nearest house on the right was a good quarter of a mile around to the other point.

Sighing at the beauty of it, Liv straightened, wrapping an arm about the patio post and resting her head against its coolness. She loved this place, loved the peace and tranquillity, the beauty of the clear aqua waters, the white sand and the untouched naturalness of it all.

She frowned, her thoughts returning to Joel's news concerning the sale of Mrs Craven's property. Just thinking about a large tourist complex or a casino in the area chilled her heart. As she saw it the Whitsunday's entire appeal was its untouched beauty.

Surprisingly, that was the one point that D. J. Denison and her father had agreed upon, the need to fight any plans to build high-rise buildings or massive tourist complexes in the area. Charles Jansen had been a fisherman who was proud of his solid working-class background, and the fact that D. J. Denison was a wealthy man filled her father with an inbred mistrust.

Not that D.J. hadn't worked to get where he was. He was fond of telling everyone he was a self-made man and he had built his business up from a one-ferry concern until he had a whole fleet of passenger ferries with the monopoly on transporting holidaymakers to the various island resorts of the Whitsunday Islands. And, of course, D.J. had wanted Ryan to become part of his empire, so that he could take over later on when D.J. decided to hand over the reins.

Liv's lips thinned. But that hadn't been enough for Ryan. To give him his due he had graduated from the University of Queensland with honours in engineering and he had taken various courses in business management. None of it seemed to satisfy him, he always seemed to be searching for something that was missing. Oh, he had stuck it out working for his father for almost a year, until that night when everything had exploded around them all.

Who could pinpoint when it had all started, the moment that steered their lives in that particular direction? Long before those few weeks, those snow-balling weeks, that led to their marriage.

With a sigh Liv sat down on the top of the short flight of steps, resting her shoulder against the railings and wrapping her hands about her knees. It was useless to try to keep these memories at bay. Tonight they crowded, surged, unsettled her. She knew she was fighting the inevitable, so perhaps if she allowed her disturbed thoughts an outlet then she could put them all behind her again, set them back into place, and that was the past. Besides, eight years was a long time, and if she couldn't think it over rationally, get it into perspective now, then she never would.

She could remember the first time she had seen Ryan Denison as vividly as if it had happened this afternoon. The moments had been etched on her mind, stored safely in her memory bank, and now the button had been pushed and she could see herself on that summer afternoon nearly nineteen years ago.

She had been six years old, and she had been riding her new bicycle to school for three days, feeling very grown-up and important. On that particular afternoon she was riding across the park, taking a short cut to the beach and her home. When four boys jumped out from behind a hedge her bicycle wobbled and it was all she could do to land upright on the path.

The boys ran around her, laughing and jeering, shoving her bicycle, and the tears coursed down her cheeks. To a six-year-old the boys were just short of being men, but she guessed they were all between ten and twelve. Wrapped in her fear and a rising anger, she began to shout back at them, unaware that another cyclist had slithered to a halt beside them and two of the boys were flat on their backs before her tormentors knew what the newcomer was about. The oldest of the boys put up a fight and by the time the four of them had disappeared her rescuer was sporting a bloodied nose and torn shirt.

Looking up at him with tears still damp on her cheeks, Liv thought he resembled all the Prince Charmings in every fairy story she had ever read. Even at twelve years old he showed the promise of the attractiveness that was to come. He wiped a hand across his nose, dimissing the smear of blood disdainfully, and began to dust the gravel and twigs from his jeans.

'Thank you for chasing them away,' she said tremulously.

'That's okay.' He pulled an almost clean handkerchief from his pocket and handed it to her. 'Here, you'd better dry your eyes.'

She did what he told her and returned his hanky. 'Thank you. Hadn't you better wipe the blood away?'

He gave his nose a cursory wipe and stuffed the hanky back in his pocket and picked up his bicycle. It was bright and shiny with all sorts of wires and attachments running all over it.

'I don't think those idiots will be back,' he said, 'but I'll ride to the edge of the park with you. What's your name?'

'Liv. Olivia Jansen.' She picked up her own bicycle and began to ride along beside him, her cycle shaking precariously.

'I'm Ryan Denison.' He eyed her riding technique. 'Haven't you been riding long?' He was matching his pace to hers and giving her weaving line a wide berth.

'No. My father has only let me ride to school since Monday. My bike's new. It was my birthday last week,' she told him proudly. 'Have you had your bike very long?'

'Years,' he grinned. 'But everyone's wobbly at the start. It took my brother months to learn to ride his bike.'

Liv's heart had swelled with pride. She had

managed to get her balance almost right away, after her father had held the seat for a while to steady her.

They were soon at the park gate and he pulled up and smiled again. 'Well, I'll see you.'

'Thank you,' she smiled back, her eyes adoring him, seeing him as her father, the brother she'd always wanted, and Santa Claus, all rolled into one.

He laughed gaily. 'You can thank me again when you're sweet sixteen, with a kiss.' His laughter followed her as, face flushed, she rode away. 'See you in about ten years, Liv Jansen,' he called after her.

Liv's lips moved into a cynical smile. He had been a precocious brat. She'd seen him on and off through her school years and she often heard her father grumbling about D.J.'s harum-scarum son and his devilry down at the dock.

Not that Ryan Denison ever seemed to notice her. While his presence across the school ground or on the beach was enough to stop her in her tracks, to stare after him, filling her with an indescribable yearning she had no way of understanding.

However, she didn't meet him to speak to until the evening she attended a friend's birthday party, three months before her own seventeenth birthday. Most of her friends from school were there and Liv had no idea that the Denison brothers had been invited to attend. The party was in full swing when Joel and Ryan arrived and Liv caught sight of them through a break in the dancers. At least, she saw Ryan. No one but Ryan.

She knew she would never forget that moment. Her breath had caught somewhere between her lungs and her throat and her heartbeats had quickened considerably. He was by far the most handsome man she had ever seen, and at twenty-three Ryan Denison had everything going for him. He was tall, dark and handsome and his family were quite wealthy and well known in the community.

If Liv thought Ryan was attractive so too did every other female at the party, and he was soon surrounded by girls. Shyly she kept to the side, watching surreptitiously as Ryan moved about from group to group. She knew when he was dancing, when he sat out to talk, and she compared him with the other young men present. She had to admit there was no comparison. To Liv he was everything the others were not.

She had been so engrossed in her thoughts that she started in surprise when Joel Denison sat down beside her and asked if she'd care to dance with him. She had accepted almost automatically, and after a few minutes Joel's easy manner had overcome her shyness and she found herself laughing and joking with him as though she had known him for ages.

That was the type of person Joel was, and she wished for the umpteenth time that she could have fallen for him instead of making a complete and utter fool of herself over his brother.

At that time, as far as Liv was concerned, Joel Denison, although a nice enough person and reasonably attractive in his own right, was simply a pale replica of his older brother. He wasn't quite as tall, not quite as broad or as dark, and he could never be as strikingly handsome as Ryan. But then handsome is as handsome does. Hadn't she had that proverb proved to her?

She had spent the next hour or so dancing with and talking to Joel and once, on the dance floor, Ryan had noticed them together. Deep blue eyes had narrowed speculatively before he turned away. The room began to get smoky and stuffy and Liv and Joel had wandered out on to the terrace, and it was here that Ryan found them when he came to see if Joel was ready to leave.

They were both sitting balanced on the patio railings and Ryan's presence was almost enough to send Liv crashing down on to the lawn a storey below.

'Hey there, careful!' Ryan's hand went out to steady her as she scrambled off the railing. Liv's mouth had gone dry and her arm seemed to burn where he had touched her. His eyes were moving appreciatively over her and he smiled slowly.

'Well now. So this is the reason I haven't seen hide nor hair of you all evening, Joel.' Ryan wiped back a lock of dark hair that had lifted in the breeze. 'Aren't you going to introduce us?'

'I know I'm going to regret it,' Joel said ruefully, 'but Liv Jansen, my brother, Ryan,' he smiled goodnaturedly at them both.

'Liv Jansen.' He took her hand, holding it firmly while a frown crossed his brow. 'I seem to remember that name.' His white teeth flashed in a smile. 'Now I know—the bicycle!' His eyes moved over her appraisingly once again. 'You've changed just a little since then, definitely for the better, too.'

Those deep blue eyes touched on the rise of her breasts and she felt herself blushing. 'I also seem to recall something else, a little pact we made. You owe me one kiss, Liv Jansen, and I think the time has come for me to collect it.'

'Hey, what's all this?' Joel put in.

'I once saved Liv from a group of teasing menaces and she promised me a kiss when she was sweet sixteen. You are sixteen?' he raised one eyebrow in amusement.

'Yes, I am. I'm nearly seventeen, but I didn't make any promises,' began Liv, her face flaming.

'Ah, Liv Jansen, you don't mean to tell me you're reneging? Well, I guess I'll just have to steal a kiss.' Before she knew what he was about he had pulled her into his arms and kissed her soundly on the lips.

From that moment on she had been his, as though that kiss had been a brand, a notice that said she was his property, and, looking back, she had a fairly assured suspicion that Ryan had been aware of the fact, too. Joel had known. She could see it in his eyes and she knew he was disappointed. But she was powerless to do anything about it.

Ryan's body against hers for those few seconds had awakened her, awakened her to adult longings that she had never even dreamed had been lying dormant within her. She had known she would be only half whole until she could feel his arms about her again, the cool firmness of his lips on hers.

The Denison brothers had come to the party together in Joel's car as Ryan's sports car was being repaired and so they both drove Liv home. She had been squeezed into the front seat between them and that short journey to the bungalow had been exquisite pleasure. She could feel the firmness of Ryan's thigh pressed to hers and his arm lay along the back of the seat.

If she had had the nerve to rest her head back she would have touched his arm. Her breathing quickened at the capriciousness of her thoughts. After all, she had really only met him less than an hour earlier.

The ball of his thumb had moved feather-soft against her bare shoulder and she turned startled blue eyes on him. His eyes met hers, enmeshing her, and she dragged her gaze downwards to settle on the masculine curve of his lips and a momentary shiver ran through her. He must have felt her involuntary movement because he smiled in an amused, almost satisfied way.

They pulled up in front of her house and Ryan unfolded himself, turning to help her out of the car.

'I'll walk you to the door,' he said calmly, and took her elbow so that she only had time to say a quick goodnight to Joel.

Her father had forgotten to leave the porch light on and she turned at the bottom of the steps. 'Thank you for bringing me home,' she had said breathlessly.

His chuckle rumbled deep in his chest. 'The pleasure was most definitely mine. And Joel's, of course.'

'Goodnight.' She turned in confusion to walk up the steps.

'I'll be seeing you, Liv,' he said quietly, and she stopped and turned, looking down at the moonlit planes of his face. His teeth flashed. 'And that's a promise.'

Recalling those moments Liv squeezed her eyes closed to try to erase the pictures her memory was flashing before her. God, she had been naïve and gullible, she thought inexorably, dismissing a fleet-ingly tolerant thought that she had been young and in love for the first time. In love for the first time? she jeered at herself. In love for the first and last time, she told herself forcefully, a band of pain encircling her heart, slipping beneath the thickened defence she had built to shield its vulnerability.

Yes, she had been ripe for his picking, like a field-mouse scampering about the cornfield unaware of the stalking, ever-watchful cat. The fact that Ryan Denison had shown an interest in her had Liv's young heart soaring with the heady ecstasy of a wedgetail on a thermal. Because Ryan Denison could have had his pick of any girl in the district.

But what was the point of bringing it all back? What possible good was it doing her? It was old history now. Sitting in the cool sea breeze, her eyes closed, Liv felt the first stirrings of tiredness. She should get up, go to bed now with the drowsiness upon her.

Her eyes flew wide open. That noise! It sounded like someone stepping on a dry twig. And was that a footfall at the side of the house? Her ears strained to each sound, her heart thundering in her head and she scrambled to her feet as a large and broad figure loomed around the corner of the patio.

'Who is it? Who's there?' Liv's voice came out high-pitched with fear as she retreated up the steps, her knuckles white as she clasped the patio post.

The figure checked his stride at the sound of her voice and then moved forward until the shaft of light streaming through the kitchen doorway fell on his face, bringing instant recognition.

Liv's hand clutched her breast over her pounding heart as its beat tripped over itself in shock. 'You!'

CHAPTER TWO

FOR the first time in her life Liv thought she was going to faint. Her body sagged weakly against the patio post and she swallowed convulsively, her throat dry and constricted. Momentarily she thought her fanciful mind had conjured him up, but he was real enough.

'My apologies for startling you.' The voice was the same, deep and resonant; she hadn't forgotten one intonation, and with painful easiness the sound of it opened old wounds she thought were safely healed. 'Well, Liv. It's been a long time.'

He was looking at her in that same bold way—and yet not in quite the same way. His eyes were in shadow, but she could feel them flowing over her, as though he had physically reached out and touched her body.

Realising she was scantily dressed in her short cotton nightdress, she wrapped her arms about herself protectively. The movement straightened her body and she drew her scattered defences about her.

'Isn't this rather late to be calling?' she asked formally, her voice sounding almost even, and she was amazed at her calmness, the normality of her words.

He raised his hands and let them fall, a cynical smile on those remembered lips. 'Is that all you can say after eight years?' He shook his head. 'A nice welcome, Mrs Denison!'

'What kind of welcome did you expect after eight

years? That I'd throw myself into your arms?' she said bitterly, scarcely believing he could be standing there.

'There was a time when you would have done just that,' he smiled evenly, putting one foot on the bottom step.

Liv made an involuntary move backwards.

'Aren't you going to invite me in?'

Dear God, if she did, the twins might waken and then . . . 'No!' The word burst from her. 'No,' she repeated, regaining a little composure. 'No, I don't think that would be a very good idea.'

He looked at her in silence for a few moments and then with one fluid movement he was standing on the patio beside her. She was not a short girl, but she had to tip her head back to look at his face, her eyes moving over his six foot one of solid maleness.

With self-revulsion she realised her body was poised, tensed, yearning for the touch of his. She almost reached out her hand to him and took a deep steadying breath. 'Ryan, I think you should go.'

'Oh. Just like that?' His lips twisted and his eyes were a flat cold steel in the bright night.

'It's late. Perhaps I could come into the village to see you tomorrow. Are you . . . will you be staying long?'

Shoving his hands deep into the pockets of his dark slacks, he turned from her to stand looking out over the water. She looked at his strong profile, trying to decide whether he had changed. His dark hair was shorter, although it was shaped neatly to the collar of his light knit shirt. If possible his broad shoulders were a little broader and even in the moonlight she could see the bulge of muscle in his forearm, as though he was no stranger to heavy manual work. His face had lost the traces of boyishness she remembered and, all in all, she had to admit he was as attractive as he had ever been.

'You've changed a lot,' he said at last, 'but then I guess we all have. Time refuses to stand still for any of us.' He swung around again. 'You could offer me a drink. For old times' sake. It's a long time since dinner.' He was looking at her.

'I . . . all right,' she said reluctantly, taking a step towards the kitchen door. 'Just wait there. I'll get dressed and bring you a beer.'

'I have seen you wearing less,' he remarked, his eyes touching the firm swell of her breasts.

The pain rose swiftly inside her, a mixture of hurt and hate, love and loss, and her eyes blazed at him. At that moment she came alive, she could have flown at him, flayed him with her fists, her nails, and her lip curled disdainfully. 'You haven't changed at all, Ryan,' she said contemptuously.

He reached her in two strides, his fingers digging into the soft flesh of her upper arms. 'And as I said, you have. My God, could someone change so much?'

'Let me go! You're hurting me!' She tried to break from his hold. 'But then that's nothing new for you, is it?'

'Liv, don't push me too far.' His words came out between his clenched teeth. For a second his hands tightened and then he pushed her away, turning from her again, his shoulders rising as he took a deep breath.

Liv stood watching him, her hands rubbing the circulation back into her arms. She knew she should go inside now, close the door on him, but still she hesitated.

'Who were the men you had here tonight?' he asked casually.

'Men? How did you know who was here and who wasn't?'

'I've been here since nine o'clock, parked along the beach. I wanted to see you alone.' He turned and looked at her. 'If you'd ended up alone.'

'Why, you . . .' she breathed deeply. 'Still judging everyone by yourself, I see,' she retorted, her face burning. So it had been Ryan in the silver car they had passed. 'And were you parked along the beach all by yourself?' she asked sweetly. 'That would have been a novel experience for the great Ryan Denison.'

His jaw set firmly. 'Look, Liv, I don't think you're creating the right atmosphere for the children. My children,' he added angrily. 'Out with one boy-friend while another boy-friend babysits.'

The blood drained from Liv's face. 'Your children?' she whispered.

He gave a negating shake of his head. 'Yes, my children. I know all about them. I've known since they were eighteen months old. Through no fault of yours,' he added sarcastically.

'How did you find out?' she asked chokedly.

'Do you care? Sufficient to say I found out.' He looked at her as though he hated the very sight of her. 'You could have told me yourself, Liv. Don't you think?' He took a step forward so that he was standing barely inches from her. 'Didn't I have a right to know?'

'Right? Right?' Her voice rose with her anger. 'You had no rights, Ryan.' Suddenly her anger burned out as quickly as it had flared. 'You didn't want any ties with me in the beginning and I didn't want any ties with you afterwards. That's all it boiled down to,' she said flatly, turning away from him. 'Now I'm tired. I'm going to bed.'

His hand snaked out and she was swung back to face him. 'You think you can wipe it all out with placebos, just like that?' He was furious. 'Try to be honest with yourself for once, Liv. You were sixteen years old, too bloody young to be tied down.'

Liv smiled calmly. 'But not too young for the other things you wanted. And that was all that counted, wasn't it, Ryan? What you wanted. And you wanted me. Well, the great Ryan Denison got what he wanted. Let's leave it at that.'

She could see that she had goaded him too far and she tried to wrench herself away from his grasp, but she was held fast.

'You think you've got me weighed up, wrapped and tied neatly in that tidy little mind of yours, branded the wicked villain. Well now, it would be a great pity to disappoint you, Mrs Denison.' He laughed harshly. 'No, I haven't changed as much as I thought I had. Perhaps I should see if you have?'

His lips came down on hers with bruising intensity, punishing, plundering and yet arousing. Strong arms slid around her, hands that went to her hips, pulling her against the rock hardness of his flat stomach and muscular thighs. Her hands were caught between them, fingers extended over his chest.

Neither of them seemed to be aware of the moment when passion replaced anger, but Liv's mind reasserted itself to find her arms had stolen around his neck, the fingers of one hand twined in the thickness of his hair. When he moved his hand around to cup her full breast she almost moaned his name.

How could she allow herself to respond to him like that after all that had happened! She felt sickened to her very stomach. But even as her mind cried out its revulsion, her body still continued its surrender. Sliding her hands back to Ryan's chest, the thud of his heart almost her undoing, she summoned what remained of her chaotic control and pushed him away.

Standing apart from him, drinking in deep clearing breaths, she watched him, feeling like a fly impaled on a pin. His face was impassive, his eyes mocking. Only the quickening of his own breathing suggested that he wasn't as unmoved by their embrace as his expression appeared to imply.

'So!' he said derisively. 'Seems you haven't changed either. We were always a matched pair.'

'Just go, Ryan,' she cried. 'And leave me alone.'

He inclined his head, an ironic smile lifting the corners of his mouth while his eyes remained cold. At the steps he turned to face her again. 'You asked how long I was staying. You'll have to get used to running into me about the place, because I'm staying. Indefinitely!' He smiled again. 'I'll be seeing you, Liv.'

And as he disappeared around the side of the house she could have sworn he added, 'And that's a promise.'

Liv closed the back door and locked it decisively. Standing by the table, she touched her cheeks to find them wet with tears and angrily dashed them away with her hand. She must have had a premonition this afternoon, some form of mental telepathy had brought Ryan into her thoughts. Why had he returned to upset her ordered life? It had taken literally years to get her life back on an even keel and now here she was floundering again in a tide of emotional upheaval. Fresh tears coursed down her cheeks.

'Mum, what's the matter?' Luke's voice came from beside her as he took her hand, looking up with sleepy worried eyes. 'Why are you crying? Aren't you feeling well?'

'Oh, Luke—no. I'm all right now, honestly.' She wiped her face on the hand towel. 'I ... I just couldn't get to sleep.'

'You can come and sleep in my bed with me if you like,' he patted her arm sympathetically.

'Oh, Luke!' She knelt down beside him and hugged him fiercely, swallowing more tears that threatened to overflow. 'Sorry I woke you up,' she said, looking into the young face with its dusting of freckles over the upturned nose. 'Want a drink before you go back to bed?'

He nodded. 'Yes, please. Mum, I thought I heard voices.'

Liv handed him a glass. 'Oh.'

'Guess I must have been hearing things.' He drank thirstily, put his empty glass on the sink and followed her down the hall.

'Sure you'll be all right, Mum?' he asked as she tucked him up again.

'Fine,' she kissed his nose. 'See you in the morning.'

The telephone's ring lured Liv from the exhausted sleep she had fallen into some time in the early hours before dawn. With a groan she turned on to her back and threw off her bedclothes. The strident ring stopped as she climbed wearily out of bed. Melly's bed was empty and she walked through to the living-room, where she could hear Luke's voice.

'She's still asleep, Uncle Joe. I think she was sick last night, so Melly and I are getting her breakfast in bed.'

'I'm awake now, Luke.' Liv ran a hand over her tousled hair, feeling decidedly jaded.

'Joel? Liv here.'

'Sorry I woke you up,' Joel sounded disturbed, 'but it's kind of important. What was wrong last night? Luke said you weren't well.'

'I wasn't sick, just couldn't get to sleep,' she said flatly. 'What was it you wanted to tell me?' She tried to stifle a yawn, refusing to even think about how the Denison family would feel about the return of the Prodigal Son.

'Hell, Liv, I don't know how to tell you this,' he began. 'Look, I think I'd better come over.'

Liv sighed. 'You can stop worrying, Joel. I already know.'

'You know? How can you know? Who told you?'

'Bad news has a habit of travelling fast.'

'But he's only just arrived,' Joel began.

'He arrived last night,' she said, wondering at the numbness that had settled over her nervous system.

'Last night? How do you . . .?' Joel stopped. 'You mean he telephoned you after I left? Was Martin still there?'

'No, Martin had gone and he actually called at the house,' she replied easily, as though their discussion concerned an everyday occurrence. She could almost hear Joel's mind assimilating what she was saying.

'He called at the bungalow? How did he know you were there?'

'I have no idea.' Liv sighed. 'Is he staying up at the house?'

'I've no idea about that either. He called to see me here at the office first. As far as I know he's gone out to the house to see D.J. now, so if you hear anything resembling a sonic boom . . .' Joel tried to laugh. 'Liv?'

'Yes, Joel?'

'I'm sorry. I never thought he'd just turn up out of the blue and I can understand how you must be feeling, but he seems to have changed a lot.'

'Do you think so?' Liv put in cynically.

'Well, yes. Didn't you think so, too?'

'No—yes—oh, Joel, I don't know.' The numbness was beginning to wear off and the return of conscious feeling was almost a pain within her. 'It was a bit of a shock, and he was—well, we didn't exactly behave rationally, I'm afraid we both said things . . . Oh, Joel, I wish he'd stayed away. I don't think I can handle it.'

'Hey, calm down, Liv.' Joel's voice was soothing. 'You can't go to pieces. It's a free country, so you don't have to see him if you don't want to. I could talk to him.'

Liv gave a short laugh. 'Could you see Ryan listening, Joel?'

'Maybe not at that.' She heard him sigh.

'And he's found out about the twins as well. He said he'd known about them for years, but he wouldn't say who told him.'

There was a short silence. 'What are you going to tell them about Ryan? The kids, I mean.'

'That's one of the things that kept me awake. I guess I'll have to tell them something. He said he'd be staying for some time and there's sure to be talk. I'd hate the twins to find out from anyone but myself.' She had lowered her voice. 'Oh, Joel! I was thinking it had all settled into the past, but it hasn't, has it? It's always there to haunt us, no matter how deeply we bury it.'

'Come on, now,' Joel was full of sympathy. 'Don't let it get you. See how things go. It may be for the best.'

'I can't follow your reasoning there.' She sighed. 'You know, you've never said a word against him, have you? He doesn't deserve your loyalty, Joel, not then and not now.' She gave a bitter laugh. 'But then I can't talk, can I? He only ever had to look at me and I . . .' her voice cracked.

'Liv, don't be upset,' pleaded Joel.

'I'm sorry, Joel, I seem to make a habit of crying on your shoulder. I don't know why you put up with it. You should give me a good clip on the ear and tell me to grow up. You're far too easygoing, and I take gross advantage of you.'

'I'll tell you when I've had enough,' he laughed. 'Look, this paperwork can wait until Monday. I'll come over and drive you into town to Luke's soccer game. We can both relieve some of our pent-up tensions cheering our team to victory.'

'That sounds like the coward's way out, but maybe you're right.' Liv knew she didn't need to be alone to ponder over the previous evening's events.

'I may not always be right, but I'm never wrong,' Joel laughed. 'See you in about three-quarters of an hour.'

CHAPTER THREE

JOEL held the doors of his Statesman de Ville open for Liv and then the twins to alight, and Liv looked up at the Denison house with the same pang of awe she still experienced even after eight years. She had first seen the house at close quarters on the night of Joel's twenty-first birthday party and its beauty had taken her breath away. It still could.

Built on a mound overlooking its own private beach, a beach that held such memories for Liv, she supposed the nearest one could come to adequately describing the house would be to say that it was a huge chalet with a wide deck all round. The ocean was to the east and the hills to the west. The sloping roof was broken by large gabled windows and the front was two storeys of thick plate glass so that the panorama of the blue Pacific and the Whitsunday Islands lay before you as you stood gaping at the grandeur. No one behind the plate glass of the huge living-room could ever be immune, could ever dismiss the wonder of that view. For Liv it was almost intoxicating.

D. J. Denison had certainly done himself proud. That he genuinely loved and cared about the area was something that won his unbending personality a firm support from others in the district. Not many people liked his overbearing singleminded business methods, but everyone admired his almost obsessional protection of the area from any commercial exploitation.

Liv and the children came to share dinner with him each Saturday night in what had developed into something of a ritual. Not that Liv minded coming. D.J. also genuinely adored his grandchildren and apart from his despotic streak he was an interesting and stimulating conversationalist and could be a very charming man when he chose to be.

When the twins were born he had been insistent that Liv bring them to live at the house, but Liv had made a stand, preferring to remain at the bungalow with her own father. At that time she wanted nothing at all to do with the Denisons. Her hurt had been too raw and new. But D.J.'s obvious feelings for the twins had made it impossible for her to deny him any access to them, and when her father had died three years earlier D.J. had renewed his pressure for her to live with Joel and himself and sell the bungalow.

It had taken all the willpower and strength that Liv possessed to hold out against D.J.'s insistence and even now, not an evening passed that he didn't make some reference to his proposal. Joel usually came to her rescue, steering the conversation away, understanding her need to be independent.

Tonight Liv faced the evening with an unusual reticence, almost a foreboding. As she stepped into the car her eyes had asked Joel if Ryan would be there, but he had simply shaken his head. And even Joel's customary bonhomie was subdued as they drove the short distance to the house.

Thomas opened the door to them with his usual smile, standing back as the twins ran ahead to the

living room to greet their grandfather. Liv passed
Thomas their jackets, for the evenings could grow
cool after the heat of the day, and Joel hung back
with her, his eyes admiring his sister-in-law's appearance.

She wore a simple dress in midnight blue, the soft
material clinging provocatively to her full figure, the
thin straps displaying her smooth tanned shoulders
while her high-heeled sandals accentuated the long
shapeliness of her legs. Her thick fair hair was pulled
softly back to the nape of her neck, framing her face,
the deep blue of her dress reflecting in the blue of her
eyes.

'Does D.J. know that Ryan's back?' she asked her
brother-in-law. 'I mean, did Ryan come to see him
this morning?'

'Can you imagine D.J. not knowing?' Joel sighed
unhappily. 'Yes, I thought Ryan was heading out
here to see D.J., but apparently he phoned him. I
don't know what was said.'

'How did he take it?'

Joel shook his head. 'Calmly, surprisingly enough.
I mean, he didn't rant and rave, according to
Thomas. I quizzed him about it,' Joel smiled. 'D.J.
just nodded and went off to his study to work, and no
one heard a word out of him all afternoon.' He put his
hand on her arm to halt her steps. 'Liv? How about
you? Are you all right about it now?' he asked watching her closely, seeing the flash of pain which momentarily dulled her eyes before she could disguise it
and he nodded sympathetically. 'You still care, don't
you?' he said softly.

'Oh, Joel! I care only that the twins don't get hurt, and I'll do anything I have to do to protect them. If that means running the gauntlet with Ryan then I'll have no hesitation in doing it, any way I know how.'

'Look, Liv, I think he may have changed,' Joel began as his father opened the living-room door.

'Olivia? Joel? What are you plotting out there in the hall?' He looked sharply at his daughter-in-law. 'Come in, come in. Pour the drinks, will you, Joel?'

They sat down in the deep luxurious lounge chairs and Joel handed Liv a dry Martini.

'Luke has been telling me his team won their soccer fixture this morning,' D.J. remarked. 'I'm sorry I missed the game.'

'Yes. It was an exciting match.' Liv sipped her drink, her mind half on her talk with Joel, wondering when D.J. would bring Ryan's name into the conversation, because his presence hung over them all like a sword of Damocles.

But D.J. made no mention of his elder son and they sat through the main course with only the twins bringing some normality to the conversation, and the apologetic entry of Thomas was almost a welcome relief. Although not for long.

That D.J.'s butler was slightly ruffled was obvious as he closed the dining-room door behind him and moved over to D.J. Even then he seemed loath to put his problem into words. 'May I speak to you outside, sir?'

D.J. frowned, but before he could reply the door was opened decisively and a figure filled the doorway. For an immeasurable moment no one spoke, not even the children, and all eyes pivoted to that figure. Liv set her knife and fork carefully by her plate, her heart skipping erratically.

He had never looked more handsome, even that afternoon so long ago when he had rescued her in the park. She experienced a compelling urge to run to him, cling to him. And then her equilibrium righted itself and she set a clamp upon those spontaneous responses, shoving them back into the past where they belonged, along with the other gifts her loving nature had generously given him and he had torn and shattered in his need to take what he wanted without stopping to count the cost.

Now he stood there, the cynosure of all eyes. He wore a pair of cream denim pants which moulded his muscular thighs and flared slightly from the knee. His shirt was short-sleeved, in the same cream denim, fitted to the waist and over his narrow hips. It was open at the neck to part-way down his chest, showing the beginnings of a mat of fine dark hair. The artificial light glinted on the gold watch band on one strong wrist.

His face was set in studied expressionlessness and his eyes scarcely flickered as they moved over each of them in turn. Joel shot an anxious glance at his father and stood up.

'Sit down, Joel.' D.J. waved him irritatedly back into his seat without looking at his younger son. 'Well, Ryan, as unconventional as ever. Are you going to join us or are you going to stand there all evening?'

Ryan inclined his head, letting the door swing to behind him.

'Bring another setting, Thomas,' directed D.J.,

motioning Ryan to the empty chair beside Joel and opposite Liv.

'I've eaten, thank you, Thomas.' Ryan spoke for the first time. 'Perhaps some coffee.'

'Yes, Mr Ryan.' Thomas moved over to the coffee warmer on the sideboard.

The twins were eyeing the newcomer with interest, slightly questioning interest, as they sensed the disturbed vibes under the surface in the room.

D.J. looked at Liv and the children and back to his son. 'The return of the Prodigal,' he said flatly. 'You should have let us know you were coming instead of taking us all by surprise.'

'Come on, D.J.! That coming from you, the master of shock tactics?' Ryan raised an eyebrow before turning to Liv. 'Aren't you going to introduce us?' he asked, his eyes challenging her, indicating the two children.

Both Joel and D.J. sat up in their chairs as Liv's hands clutched together convulsively in her lap.

'Children, this is Uncle Joel's brother Ryan. Ryan, Luke and Melanie.' She was unaware of the pleading expression in her eyes as she looked back at Ryan.

Melly smiled shyly. 'We've never seen you before. Where have you been?' she asked, while Luke was looking solemnly at Ryan. Liv could almost see his mind weighing up the stranger, dissecting a problem he knew existed but was unable to fathom.

'I've been working away,' Ryan answered. 'In Fiji and New Zealand.'

'We know where New Zealand is, don't we, Luke? Because the new boy in our class comes from there and the teacher showed us,' said Melly.

Ryan nodded. 'Fiji is north of New Zealand and east of here.'

'You seem to have done all right for yourself,' remarked D.J.

'I can't complain.'

They had barely reached the living-room, leaving Thomas to clear away, when D.J. was called to the telephone. Joel gave Liv a speculative look and before she could glean a hint of what he was about, he had borne the children away to play with an old electric train set he had assembled in what was the old nursery.

Liv moved across to the window gazing out over the ocean, her hand playing agitatedly with the thin gold chain she wore around her neck. She felt instinctively when he had soundlessly crossed the deep pile carpet to stand behind her and her heart thumped loudly in her ears.

She heard him sigh. 'I never forgot this view, the way the moonlight plays on the sand and over the water,' he said softly, as though he meant what he said.

'Yes, it is beautiful.' She tried to remain calm, matter-of-fact, telling herself to treat him as if he was an acquaintance, a casual acquaintance. But he wasn't a casual acquaintance. He wasn't a casual anything, screamed a little voice inside her.

Her eyes were drawn to the beach. She could have pinpointed the exact spot, off to the right, where they had lain together. She wanted to tear her eyes from the memories of it, but it held her almost mesmerised, while her body burned with a mixture of shame and desire.

'But of course we have reason to remember this view, don't we, Liv?' His voice flowed about her like honey, soft as liquid silk, but its tenacity entangling her in its stickiness. She swung around on him, and then regretted that she was standing so close to him and his potent maleness.

'I'd rather like to forget about that, Ryan, and I consider it bad taste and ill-mannered of you to bring it up,' she said with an attempt at contemptuous dignity.

He laughed quietly. 'Can you forget it, Liv?' He ran one finger down her arm from shoulder to elbow, raising goose-bumps. 'I haven't,' he said softly. 'I remember it with vivid clarity.'

'I'm surprised you were sober enough to recall anything,' she said scathingly, as the door opened and D.J. came in.

Ryan's jaw had set angrily, but when he turned to his father his face showed no emotion, as though he had dropped a mask over his features. They made polite conversation about everything and nothing until Liv thought she would scream.

At last she stood up. 'I think we should be getting home—it's past the children's bedtime. I'll go and fetch Joel.'

D.J. and Ryan stood up, too.

'I'd better be getting along as well,' Ryan said easily. 'I'll drop you home, Liv.'

'There's no need. Joel usually takes us home.' Liv moved towards the door, needing to escape.

'No trouble. It's unnecessary for Joel to get his car out again when mine's standing at the door.' He looked at her steadily.

'Where are you staying, Ryan?' D.J. interrupted.
'You can return here if you like,' he added gruffly,
amazing even Liv.

'Thanks anyway, D.J. I'm all right for a while.'

D.J. turned a contemplative eye on Liv and reading that speculation she felt herself blush. Surely
D.J. didn't think Ryan was staying at the bungalow?

'Why aren't you driving us home like you always
do, Uncle Joel?' asked Luke, eyeing Ryan's silver
Mercedes with an unreasonable distaste. 'You do
every other night.'

Liv flushed at her son's ill manners, even as she
agreed wholeheartedly with the sentiments he ex-
pressed.

'Mr Den . . . Ryan has kindly offered to save Uncle
Joel a trip,' she began, while the look Joel turned on
his brother was a mixture of embarrassment and sympathy. Without showing any outward concern or
making any comment Ryan opened the rear door of
the car and Melly climbed in. He leant over and
adjusted her seat belt for her before standing back to
let Luke follow her in. Luke gave him a level look
before getting into the car and he quickly buckled his
belt so that there would be no need for Ryan to assist
him. Liv subsided into the passenger seat, without a
glance in Ryan's direction. They were silent during
the short drive around the bays and Liv's nerves were
stretched tautly by the time the car drew to a smooth
halt in front of the bungalow.

'Thank you for the lift home,' said Luke, his tone
dismissing Ryan in what was almost rudeness.

Ryan raised one eyebrow. 'I'll see you inside. I'd
like to talk to your mother, if I may?' His steady look

threw Luke into indecision and he shrugged his young shoulders and turned towards the house.

Leaving Ryan in the living-room, Liv had soon organised the children into their pyjamas and after they had cleaned their teeth and said a restrained goodnight to Ryan she settled them into bed.

Melly's eyelids were drooping as Liv tucked the bedclothes around her.

''Night, Mummy. Isn't Uncle Joel's brother nice? He's so handsome!'

Liv pulled Melly's door closed, thinking ironically that Ryan obviously hadn't lost his appeal, and crossed to Luke's room. He lay tense and straight and unsmiling.

'What does he want to talk to you about, Mum? You know you don't have to talk to him if you don't want to.'

'Now why shouldn't I want to talk to him?' She leant over and kissed him. 'Stop worrying and go to sleep now.'

'Well, I don't like him,' he frowned.

'Oh, Luke . . .' Liv began.

'Well, I don't. So you just call me if you want me to come out,' he said solemnly, his set face having a fleeting resemblance to Ryan's for all that his features and colouring were Liv's.

Liv gave him a bearhug. 'All right, I'll call you if I want you. Now, everything is going to be all right. Go to sleep, love.'

''Night, Mum,' he said reluctantly.

The kitchen light was on and Ryan had two coffee mugs on the table and was about to pour boiling water on the grains when Liv just as reluctantly joined him.

'Milk and no sugar? Right?' he said without looking up. 'See, there's lots of things I remember.'

'Ryan, I'm getting heartily tired of these little innuendoes. I don't know why you're playing this cat-and-mouse game, but I don't want any part of it—and I don't want the children upset.' She looked coolly across the table at him, marvelling at the control she had over herself.

'I can understand that,' he said, sitting down at the table and motioning her to the chair opposite.

His reasonableness threw her and she sank into the chair in surprise. When he didn't elaborate she sipped her coffee perplexedly. This submissiveness was totally new to him and she was undecided about how to handle it. He drank his coffee in silence, his eyes moving lazily about the kitchen before swinging back to her.

'They're great kids. You've done a good job with them.'

'Thank you.' She couldn't completely eradicate the edge of sarcasm from her voice and she saw his lips tighten as her barb hit home.

Ryan stood up and rinsed his mug and Liv knew a moment of relief that he would leave. But he stood with his hands resting on the back of the chair, his eyes looking steadily at her. 'You never used to be sarcastic, but I guess I deserved that. I did leave you alone to face the whole thing even if I was unaware of the full extent of it. But at the time I had my reasons for leaving.'

He turned from her, flexing his shoulder muscles as he shoved his hands in the back pockets of his pants. The material of his shirt strained, the cream colour accentuating the deep mahogany tan of his muscular arms. 'I want to begin making amends, Liv.'

She stood up, a multitude of thoughts crowding her mind, a tide of emotions shaking her previous composure—anger, uncertainty, fear.

She must remain calm. 'We manage very well, Ryan. We don't need anything.'

He spun round, anger in his face, in the tension of his body. 'Damn you, Liv!' A muscle worked in his jaw. 'I don't mean that. I'm well aware that you haven't touched a penny of the money I sent to the bank.' He prowled about in exasperation. 'You're a stubborn . . .' he stopped and took a deep breath. 'I meant I want you with me, the three of you. I want to make these eight years up to you.'

A wave of yearning washed over her, only to recede once more, uncovering her hurt and rejection, and her own anger rose within her. 'Make it up to us? Make amends? For what?' She almost spat at him. 'Why, you arrogant, self-opionated . . . Do you honestly think that we need you?'

'Liv, for God's sake, think about it rationally.' He had moved round the table to stand in front of her. 'I'm not penniless. I can give the children the kind of life they should have, an education . . .' He put his hand on her arm and she slapped it away.

'Take your hands off me! My children,' she took a deep breath, 'are happy and well cared for and they're loved. Anything they need I can give them.'

'Even a father?' His eyes bore cruelly into her face and she could see he had his anger under tight control.

'Even a father,' she repeated, and added recklessly, wanting to hurt him as he had hurt her, 'Martin Wilson, a good friend of mine, has asked me to marry him and I may accept him. So you see, you needn't have made the effort to come back, Ryan. Your journey's been a total waste of time.'

'Has it?' he asked quietly, dangerously quietly. 'You're a married woman, Liv, remember? You can't marry anyone unless you plan to commit bigamy.'

'There always divorce,' she threw back at him. 'You've been gone long enough for desertion to be adequate grounds for divorce.'

'But you're forgetting one thing, Mrs Denison.' His hands rested lightly on her arms. 'I don't particularly want a divorce, especially now that I've seen what I've been missing. We have a lot of time to make up.' His head rose. 'You're mine, Liv, and what's mine stays mine. I'm taking you back, you and the twins.'

'Back?' She brushed his hands away. 'You can't have something back that was never yours to start with.' She moved towards the hall. 'I'll see you out, Ryan. We have nothing more to say to each other.'

'The hell we haven't!' His hand caught her to him and she tried to free herself, only to feel the solidness of the wall at her back, the muscular firmness of his body in front of her

'Let me go, Ryan,' she said quietly, aware of the children nearby, especially Luke, who already sensed the antagonism between them.

He smiled malevolently, moving his long body against hers, and she felt the spark of desire begin to flicker in the pit of her stomach. 'Your body tells me you don't mean that, Liv,' he said huskily, the pressure of his thighs searing through the thin chiffon of her dress. His lips touched her temple, teased her earlobe, sending shivers of bittersweet anticipation through her body. One leg insinuated itself between hers, resting there, exerting an arousing pressure.

His hand moved to the back of her head, impatiently removing the clasp at her nape, his fingers threading through the loosened thickness of her hair. 'Don't tie it back. I like it free, so I can run my fingers through it,' he murmured, bringing a handful to his face and inhaling the clean freshness of its fragrance. 'I can remember that scent. In eight years it never faded.'

Liv had to strain to catch his words, words that she was sure he was unaware he had spoken.

Both hands held her head and his lips descended to take possession with a passion that seemed to fire them both. Her lips opened to welcome his demand for a response she was returning without thought. Her hands fumbled with the buttons of his shirt, opening it so that she could feel the heady firmness of his skin. Her fingers moved through the soft mat of hair, and the blood pounded in her own ears.

With an urgency that matched her own his hand moulded one firm swell of her breast, its tautening nipple arousing him further. The snap of one thin strap of her dress dragged her back to reasoning consciousness.

'Ryan!' She pushed against his chest, putting some small distance between their upper bodies. She didn't need to be told he was as physically aroused as she was, she could feel it in the tautening muscles of his lower body, and she had to fight an almost uncontrollable urge to cast rational thought to the four winds, to just allow herself to drown in the heart-stopping ecstasy of mutual physical arousal, to seek the satisfaction she knew he could give.

But she had allowed herself to do that once before and almost wrecked her life and, in some part, his. 'Ryan, please, let me go. I think you should leave. I want to go to bed.'

'So do I,' he replied caressingly. 'With you. God, how I want to make love to you!' He drew her back into his arms again, his lips moving over her jawline. 'Mmm, you smell delicious. You taste delicious. You feel delicious,' he murmured. 'Which room is yours?'

'Ryan, I don't want to sleep with you,' she said firmly, not able to control her body's responsive shiver.

He chuckled deep in his throat. 'Liar! You want me as much as I want you. Eight years is too long— far too long.' He had manoeuvred them to the first door on the left, the room Liv shared with Melly. 'This it?' His hand moved to the door knob.

'I share that room with Melly, Ryan,' she said softly, and as his hand hesitated, 'I couldn't imagine even you wanting to run the risk of her waking up at an inopportune moment,' she said flatly.

A few seconds ticked away. 'You bitch!' Ryan muttered harshly, his hands biting into her flesh before he put her away from him. His eyes raked her face so that she almost flinched and then he strode to the door. 'Remember what I said, Liv. You are mine.' His words were soft, distinct, so that they seemed to echo down the hallway. 'You always have been mine. And I mean to keep it that way.'

*

Morning dawned bright and clear with just a hint of the heat that was to come later in the day, and for the first time in her life Liv cursed the sunshine. That the sun could shine when she felt so low and grey and bleak she could scarcely abide.

As she prepared breakfast for the three of them she felt she was walking about like an automaton, motivated by some external force which kept her body functioning after her heart and mind had ceased.

Melly chattered happily, spreading jam on her toast, while Luke nibbled morosely on his cornflakes.

'You're a slowcoach this morning, Luke,' Melly remarked. 'I'm beating you by miles.'

'I'm not racing,' replied Luke gruffly, frowning at his sister.

'What a grumpy bear you are!' She turned to her mother. 'Luke got out of the wrong side of the bed this morning.'

'Oh, shut up, Melly! Why are girls always nattering and giggling?'

'I don't natter and I don't giggle.' Melly was affronted. 'At least, not often.'

Luke gave her a withering look.

'Come on, you two, no fights,' Liv intervened. 'Eat your breakfast, Luke.'

'I'm not very hungry really.' He pushed his plate away, not looking at his mother.

'Don't you feel well?' Liv's forehead puckered.

'No—yes. I'm all right, Mum.' He picked up his orange juice and his eyes reluctantly met his mother's over the rim of his glass.

'Has Uncle Joel got any other brothers?' he asked

out of the blue as Liv turned back to lift the toast out of the toaster.

Her hand froze on the warm bread, knowing she couldn't lie to him, not blatantly like this, nor did she want to tell him the truth at this moment. Last night and her encounter with Ryan still sat too rawly on her heart for her to calmly talk to the twins about him. Dear heaven, what was she to do?

'Mum?' Luke pressed his point while Melly looked on, her eyes puzzled by Luke's question.

Liv cleared her throat. 'No. No, he hasn't.' She calmly buttered the toast and set it on the table.

Two pairs of eyes gazed at her, Melly's deep blue and innocent, Luke's a lighter blue and, all at once, almost the eyes of an adult. At seven years old? Liv asked herself. She must be reading more into his expression than was there. Such was a guilty conscience, she told herself.

'He's so handsome, isn't he? Much handsomer than Uncle Joel,' said Melly. 'But Uncle Joel's really nice, too,' she added quickly as though she thought she had been disloyal to Joel.

The telephone pealed loudly and Liv jumped up to answer it. Never before had she welcomed an interruption more.

'Good morning, Olivia.' Martin's voice answered her breathless 'hello'.

'Oh, Martin. How are you? You're up bright and early.'

'I've been up for some time.' He made it sound unhealthy to remain in bed after daybreak. 'I usually go for a jog around the park before breakfast as often as I can.'

'Very invigorating,' Liv remarked, for something to say.

'Yes, very,' he said. 'Are you free this afternoon? I thought you and the children might like to take a drive somewhere if you'd care to and aren't doing anything else.'

Suddenly to be away from the bungalow, away from any chance of crossing Ryan's path, was just what Liv needed. Perhaps it would postpone Luke's questions for a while, give her time to prepare her answers, because she knew he would ask again.

'The children will be home from Sunday School by eleven o'clock. Would you care to take a picnic lunch up the coast a way?' she asked him.

'A picnic? That sounds fine. I haven't been on a picnic since I was a youngster.' Martin sounded surprised. 'The children should enjoy that. I'll be around about eleven-thirty. That all right?'

'That would be fine. It will give me time to pack lunch. See you at eleven-thirty, then.'

She went back to tell the children about the picnic. Melly was excited even when she learned that Martin would be going along. However, Luke was a little more reticent, his eyes telling her that he had only shelved his questions until another time.

Liv was closing the lid of the cold box on their cold chicken and salad lunch when Martin arrived and they were soon in the car and on their way. Liv and the children wore their swimsuits under their shorts and cool tops, and Liv eyed Martin's long pants and shirt, shoes and socks with some amusement. Did he ever let his hair down and relax? she asked herself.

'Have you any suggestions about where we should

go?' he asked. 'I'm afraid I haven't been around much outside the township.'

'I know just the spot. The children and I usually go there for a picnic. It's a favourite of ours. There's plenty of shade and the beach is safe for swimming,' Liv told him.

'Just give me the directions,' he smiled. 'I'll leave it to you.'

The twins were paddling at the water's edge after lunch while Liv and Martin lay back on a rug on the sand under a shady palm tree. Feeling almost relaxed, Liv idly picked up a handful of sand, letting it slide slowly through her fingers. Martin's eyes moved over the attractive picture she made stretched out beside him, her white shorts accentuating the smooth even tan of her long legs, her loose red tank top gently moulding her feminine curves.

'Have you given any thought to my proposition, Olivia?' he asked quietly. Now that Martin had decided his course he wanted to begin putting his plan into action.

For a moment Liv was hard pressed to recall the proposition he was talking about, and she experienced a twinge of guilt when she looked at the intense expression on his face. 'No. No, I haven't, Martin,' she said at last. 'I haven't really had a free moment since Friday. It's not as though I feel I can make a snap decision.'

'Maybe not. Olivia, I . . .' He took her hand. 'I'm rushing you, aren't I? But, Olivia, once a course is plotted there's no point in putting it off. You need a husband, Olivia, and I know I could . . .'

'Martin, please, let's not talk about it this afternoon. Let's just enjoy the day without any serious discussions.' Liv tried to disentangle her hand and Martin held it tightly for a moment before reluctantly letting her go.

'All right. But I shan't give up, you know,' he said firmly. They sat in silence for a moment and it was Martin who broke that silence.

'Did you enjoy your evening with your father-in-law last night?'

'It was very enjoyable.' Liv was glad she could hide her expression behind her dark-lensed sunglasses. Enjoyable? Good grief! Devastating was the more operative description. She knew now was the time to tell Martin about Ryan's return, but somehow she just couldn't bring herself to mention it. It would mean a cross-examination, more explanations and more questions that would start further soul-searching, and she shied away from that like a wild pony from a bridle.

What could she say anyway? 'Oh, Martin, by the way, a funny thing happened. My husband turned up. It was quite a little family reunion. We mulled over old times.' She felt an hysterical laugh well up inside her and she jumped to her feet, taking Martin by surprise. 'Did you bring your swimsuit?'

'Well, yes. It's in the car.' Martin sat up.

'Then how about a swim now that our lunch has settled?'

'If you like. I'll have to change in the car,' said Martin, reluctantly getting to his feet.

'See you in the water.' Liv slipped out of her shorts and top, leaving them in a tidy pile with the twins' clothes, and ran down into the water, welcoming its coolness on her hot skin.

Martin joined them, a trifle selfconscious in his old-fashioned swim shorts, his skin white and untouched by the sun. His body was slightly stooped and on the thin side, and Liv found herself unconsciously comparing him with another body, tall, lithe, muscular and oh, so familiar. So familiar in fact, that she felt she knew every contour of it by heart, even after eight years. With a spurt of anger she turned and dived into the blue water, wishing that a certain dark-haired twelve-year-old boy had left her to fight her own battles all those years ago.

It was nearly dusk by the time they headed back to Shute Harbour. The afternoon had been quite successful and even Luke had rediscovered his high spirits, although both of the twins preferred to keep Martin at arm's length. He was, after all, a teacher at their school and therefore just a trifle awesome.

The day in the open air did the three of them good, because they all slept well that night, with no mention made of Ryan Denison. Neither did he call at the bungalow or telephone as Liv half expected he would. In fact, it was almost a week before she heard any more of him.

CHAPTER FOUR

EACH Tuesday and Friday Liv worked at the gift shop until five o'clock and she had an arrangement with Maria Costello for her to collect the twins from school and take them home with her own two children. Liv then picked the children up from the Costellos' house on her way home from work.

At four-thirty on Friday she looked up from the shelf she was dusting as Joel walked in. Surprisingly she hadn't seen or heard from Joel since Saturday, and usually he called in once or twice a week.

'Hi!' he smiled a little sheepishly.

'Hello, Joel. What have you been doing with yourself all week?'

'D.J. sent me down to Brisbane for a few days. I just got back this morning.'

'Oh! That was a sudden trip, wasn't it?'

He nodded and sat on a stool near her counter. 'D.J.'s still delving into old Mrs Craven's affairs, or should I say I've been delving into Mrs Craven's affairs. God, I'm sick of it, Liv!' he shook his head in exasperation. 'I'm half glad I couldn't find out anything even if D.J. is out of sorts with me.'

Liv smiled. She could imagine 'out of sorts' would be an understatement where D.J. was concerned. Nothing less than perfection was enough for her father-in-law. 'Perhaps D.J. has met his match. No doubt Mrs Craven will tell everyone all about it when she's good and ready.'

Joel gave her a strange look. 'You don't seem perturbed. I mean, in his time, your father used to get as steamed up as D.J. does over any proposed development of Craven or any other island in the area.'

'I know, Joel. And I'm not saying I want to see a huge complex built there, but after all, it is Mrs Craven's property and she has every right to dispose of it as she sees fit. She's a grand old lady and I can't see her letting anyone pull the wool over her eyes.'

'My sentiments exactly. D.J.'s just going to have to cool his temper and try his hand at patience—no mean feat for him. Anyway, enough of that. What about you? How are things?'

Liv returned his gaze. 'I presume you mean with respect to Ryan?' she said flatly.

Joel shrugged his shoulders. 'I guess so.'

'I haven't seen him since Saturday night and I don't care if I never see him again,' she said expressionlessly.

'Hell, Liv! Give him a go——' Joel began.

'A go? You can say that, Joel, after all he's done to you, to me, to D.J.?' she asked, her anger rising.

'What did he do, Liv? Except maybe want to live his own life the way he wanted to live it. He's different from me, Liv, he knows exactly what he wants from his life. He always did, even as a kid. I can compromise, bend with the wind. But not Ryan. He hasn't got a compromising bone in his body; it's all or nothing for him. I guess he's pretty much like D.J. That's why they never really hit it off for long.' Joel sighed. 'Did he say anything when he took you home on Saturday night? About his plans?'

'We talked, if you could call it that.' Liv felt herself blush at the memory and she turned away from Joel.

'I think he'd like to have you back,' Joel said quietly, choosing his words carefully.

'Oh, Joel! It's too late. Don't you see that?' Liv paced about. 'Anything I felt for Ryan—well, it died eight years ago.'

'Are you sure, Liv? Are you really sure? I think you should give Ryan a second chance.' He looked at her seriously. 'For the twins' sakes at least.'

'That's emotional blackmail,' Liv said quietly, and shook her head. 'No, Joel, I just couldn't go through it again.' She clasped her hands together agitatedly. 'I . . .' She stopped as a customer entered the shop and Joel sat quietly until they were alone again.

'I feel as if I'm caught in a cleft stick with you on one side and Ryan on the other. And I care about you both,' Joel said earnestly.

'How can you be so . . . so . . . Good heavens, Joel, I would have thought you'd be the last person to go to bat for him, to welcome him back with open arms. He never cared about your feelings either. Ryan's a taker, Joel—you must see that. What he wants, he takes, at whatever cost.'

'Takers only take what others allow them to take,' he smiled crookedly, and Liv saw a fleeting resemblance to Ryan in his face. 'Anyway,' Joel's smile faded, 'he never took anything from me that began as totally mine.' He looked at her steadily in the eyes and Liv was the first to look away.

Joel stood up and shrugged his shoulders and Liv wondered if he thought he'd said too much. Joel rarely touched on anything personal and neither did Liv to Joel. They seemed to have erected a tiny area of conversational no man's land between them over the years, although in every other respect they were the best of friends.

'Well, I'd best be getting along.' He glanced down at his wristwatch. 'You'll be closing in a few minutes, won't you?'

'Mmm. Then I'm off to collect the twins.'

'Okay. I'll see you. Say hi to the terrors.' He turned

at the door. 'Oh, by the way, Ryan didn't mention where he was staying, did he?'

'No, he didn't. I just surmised it would be at the hotel as he wasn't staying at the house.'

'I can't seem to find any record,' Joel frowned.

'Oh, well, I guess I'll catch up with him somewhere. 'Bye, Liv.'

Liv closed the shop, trying not to let Joel's words start her mind tossing over the past again, and she was soon on her way to the Costellos'. Maria and Liv had become firm friends since they had been reacquainted at the local pre-school their children had attended. The other girl was a few years older than Liv and they had recognised each other from their schooldays. Maria's son, Dino, was Luke's best friend.

Of Italian parentage, Maria was short and plump and dark and doted on her husband and two young children. Her husband, Mike, had arrived in Australia from Italy when he was a young boy and he worked as the captain of one of D.J.'s fleet of passenger ferries, as his father had before him.

The fact that Mike Costello and Ryan had been friends had been another bone of contention between Ryan and his father. Not that D.J. disliked Mike, he knew that he was competent and trustworthy at his job, but to accept Mike as a friend of Ryan's had been beyond D.J.'s class-conscious outlook.

Maria was sitting on her front steps placidly shelling peas from her garden for their evening meal while she kept an eye on the four children playing in the front yard. As Liv pulled up outside she walked down to the gate smiling a greeting.

'How's everything, Maria? Sophy over her cold?'

Liv asked as the twins went running to collect their school bags.

'Yes, she's fine now. It would have been a pity if she'd been sick for her birthday tomorrow. She's been so excited about having the three of you over for lunch that I've had trouble convincing her that she has to wait until tomorrow.'

'We're looking forward to it, too. Will eleven-thirty be all right?' Liv smiled as Maria's little daughter hurried after Luke on sturdy legs.

'Fine.' Maria also smiled fondly at Sophy. 'It seems like only yesterday that she was a tiny baby. I can hardly credit she'll be five tomorrow.'

'When she goes off to school next year you'll really feel she's growing up,' agreed Liv. 'Thanks for minding the twins. We'll see you tomorrow for lunch.'

They arrived at the Costellos' next day and as soon as an excited Sophy had opened her presents Mike took the children downstairs while Maria bore Liv away to the kitchen. That something was bothering the other girl was obvious, and Liv hoped Maria's mother, who had recently had a major operation, had not taken a turn for the worse.

'I don't quite know how to tell you this, Liv.' Maria began, a frown on her pretty face. 'Honestly,' she threw her hands in the air, 'men are so thick sometimes! I could have flattened Mike when he told me what he'd done!'

Liv smiled, trying to imagine the five foot of Maria taking the thickset five feet ten of Mike Costello on in combat. 'Poor Mike! What's he done?'

'Well, Liv, I don't know how you'll react, in fact, I don't even know if you know . . .' She stopped and took a breath. 'Liv, it's about—well, it's about Ryan.' Maria watched the smile fade from the other girl's face and she moved over to lay a comforting hand on Liv's arm. 'I'm sorry, I didn't want to be the one to have to tell you he's come back.'

'It's all right, Maria, I know already. He came to see me,' said Liv. Just when she had managed to put thoughts of him from her mind for a few hours Maria's words brought it all cascading back to churn her senses into that same whirlpool of disturbance.

Maria sighed, her dark eyes still coloured with concern. 'Oh, that's good. I was so worried about telling you. I didn't want to give you a shock.' Her voice told her relief. 'You see, Mike met him down at the harbour this morning and to top it off he's invited Ryan to lunch—today of all days! Believe me, Liv, I—that is, Mike and I, we don't want to embarrass you and I didn't want him to arrive and take you by surprise.'

'Please, stop worrying, Maria. I'm . . . I'm used to the idea of his being in the area. Ryan,' she almost stumbled over his name, 'and Mike were good friends and naturally he'd want to invite him over.'

'But,' Maria's face creased into a frown once more, 'what about the twins?'

'They've met Ryan, at D.J.'s last weekend,' Liv swallowed. 'I . . . I haven't mentioned anything to the children yet about Ryan and me so . . .' she finished lamely as Mike joined them in the kitchen.

'Have you told Liv?' he asked brusquely, trying to cover his embarrassment, and when Maria nodded he looked relieved. 'Sorry, Liv, I just didn't think. I was kind of taken aback to see him, if you know what I mean.'

'If you'd rather not see him, Liv, then Mike could ask him to come another day,' Maria began.

'No. No, Maria, you can't do that.' Liv heartily wished they could. 'There's no reason why we can't behave in a civilised manner.' Liv could almost laugh at her own words, but she knew if she started to laugh she would be incapable of stopping.

'Good.' Mike tapped Maria on the bottom. 'Did you put those cans of beer in the fridge, love?'

'Do I ever forget your beer?' Maria asked.

'Not yet, you haven't,' he grinned at her, and turned to Liv. 'Don't know how I managed without her.' His face grew serious. 'I don't suppose there's any chance that you and Ryan will get back together again?'

Liv's face paled and then coloured.

'Mike!' Maria gave Liv an apologetic look. 'I'm sorry, Liv. Take no notice of him. For heaven's sake, you're about as subtle as a hit over the head with a dead fish! Go and watch the kids, you great oaf.' She pushed her husband out of the door and began apologising again.

Ryan arrived ten minutes later in his silver Mercedes, and by then Liv's nerves had been honed to fever pitch. His appearance was very nearly a relief that the dreaded moment had finally arrived.

To the children's amusement he swung Maria around, kissing her soundly, while Maria laughed a little selfconsciously, not looking at Liv. Mike drew his children forward, a proud father.

And all the while Liv stood waiting for the ultimate moment when he would have to acknowledge her presence. Eventually he turned, his eyes moving over her, not missing one minute section of her body. She was wearing a plain light blue denim shirt and a loose cotton peasant blouse and she felt his eyes as they touched her, burning tinglingly through to her skin.

'Liv,' he smiled. 'How are you?' His deep voice sent tremors down her spine.

'I'm fine,' she replied stiltedly, and felt Luke move up beside her, eyeing Ryan steadily.

'Hello.' Melly smiled up at him with scarcely a trace of her usual shyness and Liv's breath caught somewhere in her chest at the resemblance between the two of them. In no way could Ryan be called feminine and neither was Melly anything other than a little girl, but the sameness was there, in the way they smiled, held their heads, in an expression. Liv sensed Mike and Maria's tension and this increased her own.

'Hi, Melly!' His smile turned from her to his son. 'Hello, Luke.'

'Hello,' Luke mouthed without smiling.

'Feel like a cold beer, mate?' asked Mike easily, walking into the kitchen and returning to hand Ryan a frosty can. 'Come and sit out the back in the cool while the women finish with the food.'

Liv watched Ryan's back as he followed Mike through the house. He was a good three or four inches taller than Mike and his dark slacks emphasised the taper of his hips, the latent strength in his muscular thighs, while the pale blue of his light knit shirt seemed to give his hair a blue-black sheen.

Melly, Sophy and Dino followed the men and when Luke hung back Dino turned around.

'Coming, Luke?'

'Go on, Luke,' Liv gave her son a push. 'Dinner won't be long.' She bit her lip as he walked reluctantly after the others.

'When are you going to tell them, Liv?' Maria asked quietly as they returned to the kitchen.

'I don't know, Maria. I just don't know.' Liv gave the salad she was tossing all her attention. 'I'm worried about Luke. He already resents Ryan.' She sighed. 'Well, I guess resents is too harsh a word. What I mean is, I think he realises that there's antagonism between Ryan and me and because he doesn't understand what it's about it makes him uneasy. I'll have to tell them soon, before someone else does.'

Maria nodded, her expression sympathetic. 'How do you think they'll take it?'

Liv shrugged and shook her head. 'I don't know. We've talked about . . . about their father before and they know I'm not a widow, that their father and I were separated, so I'm hoping they'll be able to accept that their father and Ryan are one and the same.' She set the servers beside the large bowl of salad. 'I know I'm a coward for putting the moment off, but I just wish he hadn't come back, Maria,' she said almost desperately. 'We were going along nicely and now everything's in an upheaval.' She looked at her friend. 'I can't understand what brought him back,' she said half to herself.

'Can't you, Liv?' Maria said softly. 'As an onlooker I used to think he cared more for you than he did for anything else in that crazy life his father wanted him to live. Maybe he came back to see you again. And the kids.'

'That's a joke!' Liv's smile was cynical. 'If he'd

cared anything about us 'it wouldn't have taken him eight years to discover it, and if he hadn't been thinking about himself he would never have left in the first place.'

Maria opened her mouth to reply and then closed it again, her eyes widening as Ryan walked into the kitchen. The small room seemed to suddenly grow smaller and more confined.

'Mike sent me in for more beer and to hurry the food along.' His smile was directed at Maria and all charm.

Had he overheard their conversation? Liv wondered, and as he turned towards her she could see the complete coldness in his eyes. Judging by the momentary flash of anger she saw in the tightening of his jaw it seemed he had heard all right. Liv shivered slightly, as though someone had walked over her grave. What did she care anyway? He knew how she felt already, and besides, it served him right. Eavesdroppers never heard well of themselves.

Little Sophy's birthday lunch passed without incident and by not looking in Ryan's direction unless she was unable to avoid it Liv managed to eat the delicious meal Maria had prepared, laugh with the children, almost convince herself that he wasn't there. But she knew he was. Her heightened senses reached out to his nearness, kept reminding her with quickened heartbeats, a tingling down her spine, a throbbing ache in the pit of her stomach, until she began to feel she must touch him or go crazy. All this she kept inside behind her schooled features, her lowered lashes.

When he exerted himself Ryan could charm birds

from the trees, and he hadn't lost the knack. Soon he had the children laughing at his stories of his life in Fiji and even Luke was reluctantly listening with an interest he couldn't hide. Only Liv refrained from asking any questions, although she stored each morsel of information away to think about later. She hadn't even known he was in Fiji, and if Joel had been aware of it he hadn't let on.

'How long have you had the *Midnight Blue*?' Mike asked, and Liv frowned, wondering if she had missed part of the conversation.

'Who or what is the *Midnight Blue*?' Maria voiced the question in Liv's mind.

'Ryan's yacht,' Mike replied. 'Didn't I tell you? The forty-five-footer down in the bay. The blue one.'

Liv's eyes met Ryan's in surprise, her mind a mass of question marks. How could he afford a yacht that size? Maybe he was part of the crew? Surely it couldn't be his? No wonder Joel hadn't been able to find his brother; he must be living on board.

'I had her built last year and sailed her up from Sydney,' Ryan was saying, his eyes moving back to Mike. 'As a matter of fact, I was hoping you could come out with me one day, Mike. Although I think I know the area like the back of my hand, it has been eight years and I'd appreciate having you go over the charts with me, give me a refresher course.'

'Sure thing, Ryan. I'd love to get at the wheel of that beauty.' Mike's dark eyes glowed enthusiastically. 'When do you want to go out?'

'Whenever it fits in with you. Bring Maria and the kids.'

Mike looked at his wife. 'Well, I'm off this weekend

and Monday. It's the first public holiday I've had off in years, and I'm not rostered off then until Wednesday and Thursday next week.'

'Well, what about tomorrow? We could stay out overnight and return Monday afternoon.' Ryan looked at Mike.

'Hey, that would be really something! What do you reckon, love?' He turned to Maria.

'It sounds like fun,' Maria smiled at them both.

'Wow!' Dino's black eyes were large with excitement. 'Can Luke come, too?'

Mike and Maria looked suddenly uncomfortable, but Ryan turned easily to Liv.

'I'd be pleased to have you and the twins along. We'll make a party of it.' His face was expressionless.

'Oh, I don't know——' Liv began.

'Oh, Mummy, please! Can we go?' Melly surprised her mother by asking. 'It would be great fun, and you know how Luke loves sailing with Uncle Joel.'

Luke's face portrayed his indecision. On one hand he felt he should hold this tall stranger at arm's length for a reason he could scarcely understand, while on the other hand he had a burning desire to sail on what must be the biggest boat he had ever seen—a forty-five-footer. Uncle Joel's yacht was big and it was thirty-five feet long. This one was longer still. 'I'd like to go, too, Mum,' he said, curiosity overcoming a slight guilt.

'That's settled, then.' Mike rubbed his hands together. 'I can hardly wait. What time do you want us at the harbour?'

'I'll check the tides and let you know. Probably around seven-thirty. I'll pick you up at the jetty at Shute Harbour.'

'Great! We'll collect Liv and the twins so she won't have to take her car.' Mike looked as excited as the children did.

'Will there be enough room for all of us?' Liv asked, looking at the second top button of Ryan's shirt. 'I mean, there's seven of us besides yourself.'

'And two crew,' Ryan replied. 'Yes, there's plenty of room. I usually sleep up on deck anyway,' he added. 'Just bring your swimsuits. I've got snorkelling gear and fishing tackle on board. Perhaps you could bring an extra couple of rugs in case it gets cool out there.'

'What about food?' asked Maria. 'I could cook a couple of chickens this afternoon.'

'No worries about food. I'm all stocked up and if we run short we'll depend on the boys to catch us a few fish for dinner.' Ryan smiled at Luke and Dino.

It was all settled.

Liv and Maria cleared away the dishes, leaving the men sitting with their coffee, and, alone in the kitchen once more, Maria looked at Liv and shook her head. 'He's changed, hasn't he, Liv? Kind of grown up is the best way I can describe it, but that's not exactly it. Ryan was always sure of himself. Now he seems more—well, more human.' Maria pulled a face. 'I guess I'm not very good at expressing myself, but when I knew him before Mike and I were married I'm afraid I didn't like him very much. He was always so mocking and cynical and kind of arrogant, as though everything bored him. He's not a bit like that now.'

'Maybe now he's learnt he gets better results by smoothing it over with a lot of charm,' Liv said drily.

'Do you think so, Liv? Well, you must admit he's as handsome as ever.' Maria rinsed the last plate and when the other girl made no comment she turned to her apologetically. 'I'm an unthinking fool to rave on about him like this. I suppose it's hard for you to— well, to see him again.' Maria dried her hands on her apron. 'Are you going to come sailing tomorrow? I mean, we could stay home and just Mike could go if . . .'

'Oh, no! Maria, don't be silly.' Liv hastened to reassure her. 'You hardly ever get a free weekend with Mike on the shifts he works. I wouldn't dream of spoiling it for you, and the twins seem keen to go, too.' She tried to smile. 'I'll keep out of the way as much as possible. It's only when we're alone that we,' she felt herself blushing, 'that we start arguing.'

'Maria, where's those old football photos of Ryan and me?' Mike's voice came along the hallway accompanied by sounds of a disarranging and fruitless search.

'I'd better go and find them before Mike wrecks the living-room,' sighed Maria. 'Be back in a minute to help you finish off the dishes.'

Liv absently picked up another plate and began to wipe it slowly. What had she got herself into? Two days on a yacht with Ryan would stretch her endurance to its limits, and she wished now that she could back out of the arrangement. That would be the most sensible thing to do.

Since when have you ever acted sensibly when Ryan was around? she asked herself derisively. The twins would be disappointed if she decided they couldn't go. And she wouldn't allow them to go alone. She frowned. If she explained . . . Liv sighed. Luke would so enjoy it. He loved going sailing with Joel and maybe their mutual love of the sea would overcome Luke's antagonism towards his father. Not that she wanted Luke to grow too attached to Ryan. Oh, God, that was hardly fair. What a tangled situation!

'You've dried that plate three times,' a deep voice startled her out of her tortured reverie. 'You'll wipe the pattern off it if you keep that up.'

Liv set the plate on the table and picked up another.

'For God's sake, Liv,' he bit out quietly, 'you could acknowledge that I'm here, look at me, at least. You've been religiously ignoring me all afternoon.'

She raised her eyes and let them rest on him. 'Does that satisfy you?' Her voice was flat and she raised her eyebrows coldly.

'No, it doesn't!' He took a step towards her and Liv backed around the table. 'You will persist in provoking me and you'll do it once too often. Then I promise you I won't be responsible for my actions.'

Liv continued to watch him coldly while her heart fluttered unevenly in her breast. 'Were you ever?' She set the plate down with a clatter. 'Look, Ryan, we're both guests of Mike and Maria and I'd rather not make a scene and upset them, so kindly leave me alone,' she said emphatically.

He bowed mockingly. 'As you wish, Mrs Denison,' he said sarcastically, 'but I'd appreciate it if you didn't discuss our,' he paused insolently, 'relationship with Maria, or anyone else for that matter.'

So he had overheard her conversation with Maria before lunch. 'I haven't discussed anything with Maria that isn't common knowledge in the district.' Liv smiled crookedly. 'It was a pity you missed the speculation, after you left. Surely you can't have forgotten how often you provided such colourful food for gossip, Ryan? You used to have everyone avid for all the details of your latest escapade and our little exploit—your finest, I think,' she added acidly, 'provided more than its share of speculation, even though our fathers did try to gloss it all over and sweep it under the mat.' All the hurt and humiliation of that time flooded back and drove her on. 'Or maybe it could be better described as shoving it into a cupboard and letting it decompose into the family skeleton.'

'You . . .' Ryan went to step around the table, his eyes ablaze with anger.

'Oh, Ryan.' Maria stopped just inside the kitchen, 'Mike's taken his scrapbook out the back looking for you.'

Ryan had stopped at the sound of Maria's voice and Liv could see him forcing his tensed muscles to relax. 'Yes, I'd better go after him. Nothing like a jaunt back into the past to get a few laughs,' he said easily, and left the room.

Maria's gaze moved from the empty doorway back to Liv's flushed face. 'Phew! The air's so thick in here you could cut it with a knife. What made him so angry?'

Liv shrugged. 'Me, I'd say. I'm sorry, Maria. I guess it's a classic case of the irresistible force meeting the immovable object.'

CHAPTER FIVE

Liv climbed back into the back of the Costellos' station wagon next morning with a feeling rather akin to numb acceptance. On the drive around to the jetty the children were talking excitedly while the adults sat lost in their own thoughts. Liv felt rather as if she had been put through a wringer. Meeting Ryan at the Costellos' had been only the beginning of an emotionally draining afternoon and evening.

About half an hour before Joel was to collect them for dinner Martin had telephoned to ask them to go driving the next day. When Liv had refused, telling him they were already going out, he had disgruntledly delved to find out where and with whom they were going. Irritatedly Liv had only said they were going sailing with the Costellos. This prompted him to ask when the Costellos had bought a boat, and Liv realised that it had been the moment to explain to him about Ryan. And now she despised herself for letting the chance pass by once again. They were going on a yacht belonging to a friend of Mike's, she had told him, knowing the situation was going to catch up with her but not being able to do a thing about it, and she hated herself for it.

As usual Joel had collected them the evening before and they had spent a few hours over dinner with D.J. Ryan was not mentioned until they were about to leave and neither did he put in an appearance, although Liv had expected him as every moment passed. Surprisingly it had been Luke who brought up his name, telling his grandfather about their proposed two days' sailing. Although he directed one shrewd weighing look at Liv's face, D.J. had not referred to his son, but she wished she knew just what he was thinking about them.

It was impossible to discuss Ryan with Joel on the journey home with the children in the back, but Joel did say he had caught up with Ryan down at the harbour while he was talking to Mike that morning and that the yacht was a beauty.

And when she was safely home, without setting eyes on Ryan Liv had been perversely annoyed, for reasons she refused to analyse. Her anger had even been directed at her brother-in-law. Sometimes Joel was too good to be true. He had sat and raved about Ryan's yacht in admiration, with not a covetous bone in his body. It was a wonder Joel didn't get trampled underfoot in the business world. She had sighed, thinking everyone liked him too much to put him down.

She had tossed and turned restlessly, pieces from the past rearing up to tease her, and now here she was, about to spend two whole days with Ryan. It was the last thing she should be doing, knowing how easily he could bend her to his will.

They were drawing to a halt at the wharf and Liv's gaze fell on the graceful lines of the yacht as it rose and fell on the slight swell, and it took all her courage to climb out of the car and collect her things together. Suddenly she felt vulnerable and all the fight momentarily ebbed out of her.

Mike parked and locked the station wagon and by the time he had joined them three people had appeared on the deck of the yacht. Ryan stepped over to the rail and in his faded denim shorts, his bare chest glistening in the sunlight, and his hair lifting in the breeze, he had very much the same effect on Liv's undefended senses as he had had all those years ago at the party when he outrageously claimed his kiss. For immeasurable moments she stood quite still and watched him, the pain inside her intensifying until it was almost unbearable.

How long she would have stood there transfixed she didn't know, but Luke's preparation to jump across on to the deck of the yacht shook her out of her immobility. She was shaking as she put a restraining hand on his arm, holding him back, and she quelled the urge to berate him for his foolishness, to let out some of the suppressed emotions that churned inside her. But she could scarcely take it out on Luke.

It was Ryan who spoke. 'Take your time, Luke. We'll have the gangway in place in a moment.'

A young Fijian came forward, his white teeth flashing in his brown face, and he took hold of one end of the short gangway and sprang surefootedly ashore. He held the gangplank steady while they filed on board.

Another figure was standing leaning nonchalantly against the railings on the other side of the deck, a young girl dressed in a microscopic bikini of bright red. Long-limbed and lithe, she had skin the colour of light coffee, a shade lighter than that of the young man, who was by now lashing the shipped gangway into its position on the deck.

Ryan reached out and took Liv's carryall from her hand. 'I'll show you where you'll bunk down,' he told them. 'Oh, meet my crew, Alesi and Roko Sukuna.'

The introductions made, they moved after Ryan down into the main cabin, almost opulent enough to be called a stateroom. It was furnished in shades of blue, very fitting, as the name plaque, *Midnight Blue*, suggested.

Mike sighed appreciatively. 'Very nice, mate. Very nice indeed.'

There was a small galley and two self-contained cabins, one up forward and one in the stern, as well as an alcove containing double-decker bunks.

'You and Maria can have the four-berth cabin up forward, Mike, and Liv and the twins can take the stern cabin. Alesi has the alcove,' said Ryan.

'When I don't sleep up on deck with Ryan and Roko,' she smiled familiarly at Ryan.

Liv could sense the quick look Maria sent in her direction and she turned and poked her head into the galley, feigning an interest she didn't feel. If Ryan chose to console himself with the young Fijian girl it was no skin off her nose. She knew he wasn't the stuff monks were made of and she really didn't care, she told herself firmly, ignoring the tiny flash of something that implied she was protesting too much.

'Mind the step down,' Ryan's voice was behind her, and she moved past the galley and down into the stern cabin.

It was even more luxuriously appointed than the main cabin and contained two large berths, with a door leading off to its own shower and toilet. Luke and Melly bounced on one of the beds and Liv turned to take their bag and rugs from Ryan. He was stand-ing watching her, closer than she expected him to be, and her awareness of him seemed to expand and fill the confined space of the cabin. That he was consci-ous of the charge of electricity that sparked between them was apparent in those deep knowing eyes, and she stepped hurriedly away from him, putting the rugs on the nearest bed.

'You and Melly can have the bunks in here and Luke can take the upper bunk in the alcove. Alesi won't mind,' he said evenly.

'Thank you. Melly can share with me and Luke can have the other bed, then we won't put anyone out,' Liv replied just as evenly.

'You won't be putting anyone out. Alesi rarely uses her bunk. She likes being up under the stars,' he said.

'No doubt,' Liv replied drily before she could stop herself.

Ryan regarded her for a moment, then turned out of the doorway. 'Come up on deck and we'll get the kids into their lifejackets before we cast off,' was all he said.

'Gosh, Mummy, isn't it beautiful?' Melly was stroking the furry purple bedspread and wriggling her bare toes in the deep pile carpet.

'It's a bit sissy, isn't it?' Luke gave the room a disdainful inspection. 'I bet we won't be able to wear our wet togs down here.'

Liv gave him a reproving look and he grinned cheerfully. 'It's okay, I guess. He must be pretty rich, mustn't he? I mean, Uncle Joe's rich—one of the kids at school said so. And this boat's even bigger than his.'

'Come on, let's go up on deck.' Liv shook her head and sent them up before her.

The four children were soon tied into their lifejackets and Ryan impressed on them not to run about the deck and explained to them why they would have to wear a harness if the sea became rough. The thought of any of them falling overboard was uppermost in both Liv's and Maria's minds as they sat back out of the way and watched as Roko cast them off from the wharf and Ryan spun the wheel to steer them towards the open sea.

They made their way out of the harbour under motor power, but once past the headland the sails went up and as they caught the stiff breeze Ryan killed the engine and the throbbing of the diesels underfoot was replaced by the creak and rattle of the rigging. They cut through the clear blue water at a steady pace with all the exhilaration of skimming freely before the wind.

Stretching her bare legs out to the sun, Liv sighed appreciatively, in that moment glad she had come along. She wore a pair of dark shorts and a loose top over her bikini and she had tied her hair back in two pigtails. The breeze caught one and she brushed the thick fair strands from across her face. Maria sat beside her with Sophy on her lap and smiled her enjoyment.

'The boys are having a good time,' she laughed, 'the big boys, I mean.'

Liv turned towards the steering wheel where Ryan and Mike were instructing Luke and Dino in the basics of steering the yacht. After a while Roko took over the wheel with the boys and Mike and Ryan disappeared below to consult the charts.

Alesi sat down opposite Maria and Liv, her dark eyes moving enigmatically from one to the other. 'I didn't think anywhere in Australia could be as beautiful as where I live in Fiji, but this comes very close.' She smiled, and Liv had to admit that she was a quite startlingly attractive girl with her curling dark hair and smooth dark skin. 'Ryan always said it was breathtaking, but I'm afraid I didn't believe him.'

'Yes, it is beautiful,' replied Maria happily. 'I'm glad Mike didn't want to move away after we were married. So many young people do.'

'Like Ryan did,' the other girl nodded. 'How long have you and Mike been married?'

'Eight years now, although it makes me feel old to admit it,' laughed Maria.

Alesi nodded and turned to Liv. 'And what about you? Liv, isn't it? Such an unusual name.'

'It's short for Olivia,' Liv told her, searching for a topic to turn the conversation into safer channels.

'Oh, yes, Olivia. Very nice,' smiled Alesi. 'And I suppose you must have been married about the same time, as your little boys are the same age. Does your husband work on the sea as well?'

Liv heard Maria catch her breath. 'No,' she replied. Obviously Ryan hadn't told his two friends about her or the twins. 'My husband and I are separated,' she told the other girl, not meeting Maria's eye and feeling decidedly cowardly once again.

'Oh, that's too bad!' The look she turned on Liv was sharper, almost calculating. 'Are you a friend of Maria's?'

'Yes. We've been friends for years.'

'We were all friends years ago before Ryan left,'

said Maria, stretching the truth somewhat.

Alesi Sukuna's eyes settled back on Liv, assessing, while Liv smiled to herself, wishing she had the nerve to come straight out and reassure this girl that any relationship Alesi had with Ryan was in no danger from her. Alesi was welcome to him.

'Mummy, can I have a drink, please?' Melly's interruption was most opportune and Liv stood up and, taking her daughter's hand, walked down the narrow steps into the cabin.

Mike and Ryan looked up from the charts they were poring over.

'Just getting Melly a drink,' she said.

'There's some soft drink in the fridge opposite the galley.' Ryan went back to his charts.

Out of the blue Liv had a vivid picture in her mind of Ryan with his arms around the young Fijian girl, and the pain in the region of her heart took her completely by surprise. Surely she couldn't be jealous? she asked herself as she watched Melly sip her drink. Not after all this time. The boat rolled gently and Liv spread her feet, adjusting her stance to the undulating movement, and out of the corner of her eye she watched Ryan's dark head bent over the chart spread out on the table.

She allowed her eyes to move over the firm line of his jaw, the way the lock of dark hair fell over his brow, and the slight curl at the ends lifting it away from his neck. From this angle his long dark lashes appeared to be resting on his cheek and the muscles in his bare shoulder rippled as he moved to point something out to Mike, his other hand absently rubbing the light mat of dark hair on his chest.

Liv's eyes were riveted on him. She was incapable of looking away, and suddenly she didn't want to. A tingling sensation began in the pit of her stomach and spread its warmth all over her body and the air between them crackled again.

As though he felt her gaze on him Ryan turned his head and his dark blue eyes met hers across the space of the cabin. The years rolled away in that moment and they were two children again riding through the park, one pair of eyes bold, older than their years, and the other pair adoring. Then their eyes were meeting across the dance floor and were moving closer, close enough to merge in a kiss. They were two people running along the sand, swimming through the blue water, racing along a beach road in an open sports car with the wind tearing at their hair, strolling along arm in arm, sharing an earth-shattering look across an intimate dinner table. And they were two bodies, their surf-dampened skin highlighted by the moonglow, lying on a beach locked in each other's arms, uncaring of the passage of time, the consequences of their actions.

Oh, God, why had things turned out so disastrously? Liv's knuckles grew white where she clutched the edge of the bench. She felt tears rush to her eyes and threaten to spill on to her cheeks and in that moment she thought she saw her own anguish mirrored in Ryan's eyes.

'Mummy?' She became aware of Melly's hand on her arm. 'Mummy, I've finished.'

Liv tore her eyes from Ryan's and turned away to rinse Melly's cup and return the container of soft drink to the refrigerator. Ryan's attention had returned to his charts and as she passed him he didn't look up. Back on deck her thoughts swung in limbo as she tried to put that emotion-charged encounter out of her mind. So steeped in her own thoughts was she that they had almost reached Craven Island before she was even aware that the island had appeared on the horizon.

Ryan and Mike were back at the wheel and Roko was standing in the bow. As they drew near the island Alesi sat up from her position on the foredeck where she had been sunbathing.

Craven Island looked exactly as a tropical island was expected to look, growing out of the blue waters, all green foliage with a skirt of white sand. One end of the island was more densely covered with trees than the other end and a rickety old jetty crawled out into the deeper water from the glaring white sand of the beach.

Whoever had purchased the island from old Mrs Craven had made a good buy, no matter what the price. Being an inner island of the Cumberland group it was somewhat protected from the open Pacific Ocean by the larger, more easterly islands and the channel to the jetty was deep and clear and relatively straight, giving easy access by boat.

A flurry of birds left the trees for the safety of the clear blue sky, crying raucously as the yacht approached their domain. Roko and Ryan had lowered the sails in swift precise movements and with Mike at the wheel the diesels burbled to life as they neared the jetty. There was a gentle nudging of the rubber tyre-protected jetty posts and then Roko had jumped on to the jetty and made them fast.

Surely Ryan didn't intend they should go ashore? Obviously he must be unaware that Mrs Craven no longer owned the island, had sold out, and a clean newly painted 'No Trespassing' sign had been erected conspicuously on the jetty. Mike was lifting the children across into Ryan's arms and he turned to hurry Liv and Maria, holding them steady so they could step ashore.

Standing on the uneven planks waiting for the sensation of movement to abate, Liv turned to Ryan. 'Should we be going ashore? I mean,' she indicated the sign, 'we're trespassing.'

'Can't see anyone about to enforce the law.' Ryan's white teeth flashed. 'Besides, old Mrs Craven never minded me coming here years ago.'

'But she's sold out,' Liv told him. 'Joel told me. And your father was ...' She stopped, realising everyone was looking at her and that perhaps the information she had just passed on was confidential.

'D.J. was livid?' Ryan finished for her, unperturbed. 'I can imagine.' He turned and led the way along the jetty. 'We can swim here by the jetty where it's not too deep for the kids.' And he walked arrogantly past the official-looking sign with total disregard.

Standing on the beach, Liv looked at Maria, who shrugged her shoulders and began to slip off her shorts and top to reveal a black one-piece swimsuit beneath. 'Sounds like a great idea. The water looks divine and very inviting.'

They helped the children undress and Liv followed them down to the water. Her blue bikini was quite circumspect as bikinis went and covered twice as much of her body as the Fijian girl's bikini did, but she felt almost naked as Ryan's eyes watched her approach the water.

While the others were snorkelling out in the deeper water, Liv and Maria walked along the beach with the children, collecting tiny perfect shells. At the other end of the sweep of beach in a small clearing was a rough shack, now boarded up, bearing another 'No Trespassing' sign, and Liv said almost to herself, 'I wonder who the new owners are?'

'I've no idea. What makes you think there's more than one owner? Maybe it's someone who won the Pools.' Maria shaded her eyes from the sun. 'Mike said your father-in-law nearly blew a fuse when he heard about the sale.'

'D.J.'s very good at blowing fuses,' laughed Liv.

'You know, this place brings back happy memories for me,' mused Maria. 'We used to come here for beach parties when I was a teenager, before Mike and I were even engaged. Ryan used to bring us over in his boat, just like he has today. It was great fun. We used to send Ryan to ask Mrs Craven's permission because he could always talk anybody into anything.'

Liv pursed her lips bitterly. She knew all about that.

Maria was looking at the old shack and she laughed reminiscently. 'One time he brought Mrs Craven with him as his date. She must have been in her sixties then and Ryan gave her a fantastic time. She went for a swim and helped with the barbecue. We'd caught some fish and she showed us how her husband used to cook them in leaves over the fire. And she even did the twist in the sand. Can't you just see it?' Maria shook her head. 'That was one of the best trips we ever made over here. I think we all lost our hearts to Mrs Craven that day. She's not really the old termagant everyone says she is.'

'No. I think she just speaks her mind,' agreed Liv. 'Anyway, she's always been nice to me.'

'Me, too. After that weekend she said we could come over to the island any time we liked, so I wouldn't be surprised if Mrs Craven lost her heart to Ryan as well. But then every girl between six and sixty in the district did that at one time or another.' Maria glanced quickly at Liv and flushed slightly. 'Sorry, Liv, I do rattle on.'

Liv gave a short laugh. 'It was all a long time ago and Ryan was too nice-looking for his own good,' she tried to make a joke of it.

'Mmmm. And he still is—good-looking, I mean.' Maria watched Liv closely. 'More so, don't you think?'

Liv shrugged her shoulders, finding a deep interest in a shell she held in the palm of her hand.

'He must have done very well for himself,' continued Maria, 'having the yacht and all. Mike said D.J. disowned him when he left.'

'He had some money left to him by his mother's family,' Liv said absently.

'I wonder what he's been working at all these years? Whatever it was he must have made a success of it.'

Liv nodded. 'We should be getting back. It's almost lunch time.'

With lunch behind them, the men, accompanied by Alesi, set off to walk around the headland to a particularly good fishing spot which Mike and Ryan remembered and Liv and Maria didn't have to coax the children to take an afternoon nap. They were sleepy from their swim and the excitement of their trip and even Luke was soon sound asleep.

Perversely Liv was unable to settle and as Maria had dozed off she slipped back into her now dry bikini and spread her beach towel on the upper deck to sunbathe. She rubbed some protective screening lotion into her skin and relaxed on her back.

The boat was barely moving and the only sound came from the gentle movement of the rigging in the breeze and the occasional cry of a gull overhead. After a time Liv rolled over on to her stomach, undoing the top of her bikini so that she could get an even unbroken tan. There was no one about to see her save Maria if she awoke and the men would be away fishing for some time. She would see them in plenty of time when they rounded the headland.

She rested her head on her arms and the sun's warmth accompanied by the gentle undulation of the yacht worked their own magic; her eyelids drooped and she slipped into a light doze. She stirred slightly as the boat gave a sudden lurch, then settled back, her eyes closed.

A feather-soft touch running slowly down the length of her backbone made her eyes fly open. Over her shoulder her blinking gaze met Ryan's as he grinned mockingly. Liv went to roll over, away from him, belatedly remembered her loosened bikini top, and her fingers struggled to retie it.

The ends were taken from her trembling fingers and he paused as he was about to fix it in place for her. 'You can leave it off if you like,' he said quietly.

Her lips tightened and she glared at him.

'Okay, just a thought,' he smiled ruefully, and tied the strings in place.

'What are you doing back here so soon?' Liv's voice sounded harsh in her ears, even though she spoke softly so as not to disturb Maria or the children.

Ryan grimaced. 'I came back for another fishing reel. Alesi's jammed and we thought it would be quicker for me to fetch another reel rather than strip and free the other one, especially when the fish are starting to bite. I left her using my gear in the meantime.'

Liv raised her eyebrows, making sure she kept her gaze away from the bronzed firmness of his muscular body. He was crouching down beside her, leg muscles flexed, far too close for her peace of mind, and she longed to move further away, put more space between them. But she knew he would notice, guess her reason for moving, and she could imagine the mocking expression such a movement would evoke.

'Well, hadn't you better get the reel?' He motioned towards the reel lying beside him on the deck.

'Well, don't keep Alesi waiting while the fish are biting,' she said, unable to prevent the edge of sarcasm in her voice.

'What's that supposed to mean?' he asked, his eyes watching her, his jaw set.

'Why, nothing. What should it mean?' Liv's eyes blinked away from his face and back again.

His mouth lifted at the corners. 'Not jealous, are you, Liv? Come to think of it, your eyes have got just a hint of a greenish tinge.'

'I'm not jealous of anyone or anything where you're concerned, Ryan,' she flashed at him angrily. 'And the sooner you get that into your mind the better it will be for both of us!'

She went to lever herself upright, but he moved faster. Her hands were pinned by her sides, held to the deck, and his body loomed over her, cutting out the sun.

'Let me go!' she bit off through clenched teeth, her eyes skipping over the light mat of dark hair on his chest, the ripple of muscles rigidly tense, the firm flatness of his midriff and the fine line of dark hair disappearing into the waistband of his faded salt-stained denim shorts clinging low on his hips.

'You mouth tells me to go,' he said huskily, his eyes bright as blue sapphires, 'but your eyes ask me to stay.' And his lips moved with deliberate slowness down to her shoulder, warm and salty from the sun and sea, as he balanced himself easily on his hands and knees.

The fire flowed through her body until her flesh flamed while his lips nuzzled her skin, moving from her shoulder up to her earlobe, along the line of her jaw. And her lips throbbed in anticipation of his kiss. She was as capable of convincing the sun to cease shining as she was of preventing her head from turning to meet his lips.

It began as a punishment, a tease, but even Ryan was caught unawares by the passion that rose to engulf them both, and they clung together, the weight of his body now almost covering her, their hands moving eagerly as though they couldn't touch enough of each other.

Ryan's leg moved between hers, the hardness of his thighs waking an answering response deep within her, and she arched her body against him, lost to the physical affinity between them.

'Ryan?' His name tumbled from her as his lips followed the softness of her skin down where her bikini top began. He lifted her a little and the top came loose. 'Ryan, this is madness.' Her words ended in a soft moan as his lips covered a tautening nipple.

He lifted his head, his lips softly sensual, his eyes looking burningly into hers, a question in their blue depths.

Liv began to shake her head from side to side. 'No, Ryan! We can't ... Maria ... the children might ...'

'Come ashore with me.' His words were low and liquid, deep in his throat, his lips returning to tease hers, gently persuasive.

Liv's resistance rose and fell and faded away completely and Ryan had raised himself on one elbow, was about to stand up and pull her after him when Maria's head appeared from below deck.

'Liv?' she called quietly, and stopped when she caught sight of Ryan, his body shielding most of Liv.

Horrified at what she had almost done, how close she had come to letting herself down completely, Liv struggled to tie her bikini top, her face pale as she realised just how incapable she had been of resisting Ryan's assault on her vulnerable senses. Ryan's body remained tense as Liv sat up from behind him.

'I'm here, Maria,' she said breathlessly, feeling a blush creep up over her cheeks.

'Oh!' Maria was assessing what she saw, taking

in Liv's flushed face and Ryan's tense mouth.

'Liv, come with me.' Ryan turned back to her and whispered so that Maria couldn't hear, his fingers gently rubbing her hand as it rested on the deck between their bodies.

She looked down into his still aroused expression and her hearbeat accelerated again. But she steeled herself, setting her mouth angrily, and standing up, she walked towards Maria without a backward glance.

'Ryan was just leaving. He came back for a reel for Alesi,' she said jerkily.

'I thought I'd make a pot of tea,' said Maria, her eyes moving once again from Liv's now pale face to Ryan's tightened jaw and clenched fists. 'Would you like a cup, Ryan?'

For a moment it seemed he would ignore her question, but he sighed and stood up with one lithe and fluid movement of his highly toned muscles. 'No, thanks, Maria. I'll get back.' He snatched up the reel and swung off along the jetty without looking in Liv's direction.

Her eyes followed his retreating form for a moment, then she turned deliberately away, following Maria down into the cabin.

'Liv, I'm sorry. I hope I didn't interrupt anything,' Maria began now that they were alone.

'Of course not, Maria,' Liv replied gaily. 'Where's that cup of tea you were talking about?'

Maria stood regarding her friend across the cabin and Liv's eyes were the first to drop. 'You don't have to pretend with me, Liv,' she said quietly. 'You're still in love with him, aren't you?'

Liv turned angrily back to face Maria, but the other girl's sympathetic expression doused the angry retort and she slumped, shaking her head. 'You couldn't be more wrong, Maria,' she said flatly.

'No? Seems to me you were both giving a pretty good impression of loving,' Maria dimpled.

'Loving?' Liv turned her face away to hide the colour that rushed to her cheeks. 'It wasn't love, Maria. More like good old-fashioned lust.'

Maria chuckled delightedly. 'Sounds like fun!'

Liv expelled a breath in exasperation and when Maria winked audaciously a reluctant smile lifted the corners of her mouth. 'I knew I shouldn't have come along on this trip, Maria,' she said unhappily. 'I had a feeling something like this would happen.' She sat down shakily at the table and put a trembling hand to her head. 'I haven't had a moment's peace of mind since he came back.'

'But surely you knew he would return eventually?' Maria sat down opposite her.

'I suppose I've never allowed myself to think about it. I wish . . .' Liv stopped, squeezing her eyes tightly closed against the memory of those moments in his arms.

'Don't you think you could make a go of it, Liv?' Maria asked earnestly. 'If you still have just a spark of feeling for each other it's worth a try, surely?'

'No.' Liv shook her head. 'I . . . he . . . The Ryan Denison I fell in love with didn't exist outside my imagination. I realised that eight years ago. Oh, I know I built him up into something of a god and I know it wasn't entirely his fault that he couldn't match up to that image, but he didn't even attempt to

. . . He never wanted to marry me in the first place.'

'But he did marry you,' put in Maria.

'Only because D.J. and my father pressured him into it,' Liv retorted bitterly.

'He wouldn't have married you if he hadn't wanted to, Liv. Heavens, Ryan would have been the last person to be forced into taking that kind of step if he'd been dead set against it.' When Liv made no comment Maria stood up and walked into the galley. 'I'll make that cup of tea.'

For a few moments Liv sat dejectedly at the table and then, with a sigh, she stood up to collect the cups for their tea. As she stepped out from the table her foot caught the edge of a rolled chart that had obviously fallen underneath and she bent down to retrieve it. It must have been one of the charts Ryan and Mike had been studying earlier.

Curiously she unrolled one end of it, expecting to see a maritime chart of local waters, but it seemed to be more of a blueprint. Liv laid it on the table and sitting the sugar bowl on one end to keep it down, slowly spread it out flat. The bold print on the bottom leapt out at her! Ryan Denison Enterprises. With an address in Auckland, New Zealand.

It looked like a floor plan, very detailed, of what appeared to be a chain of small buildings joined together to form a whole settlement.

'What's that?' Maria had walked up behind Liv and peered over her shoulder.

'I've no idea.' Liv bent closer. 'I found it under the table. It seems to be some sort of,' she stopped, 'chain of small cottages. See here, each of these appear to be self-contained units. And here's a pool,' Liv pointed out, 'and a tennis court. It looks like some sort of tourist complex.' Her breath caught in her throat and she turned to Maria, whose expression mirrored her own. 'You don't suppose . . .?'

'Unroll it a bit more.' Maria took the rolled end and spread it out on the table so that they could get an overall picture of the whole project. Her finger traced the rough outline of the property. 'It could be Craven Island, except that there's part of the end by the shack cut off.'

Searching through the other charts, Liv eventually found the one she was looking for and held it open for Maria to see. 'It is the island,' she said incredulously.

'But what would Ryan be doing with plans for building a resort here on Craven Island? He'd have to own the island to . . .' Liv stopped.

'Liv, is it possible?' Maria asked with utter disbelief.

Liv shook her head. 'I can't believe it. How could he possibly be able to afford to buy the island? And how did he manage to talk Mrs Craven into selling to him when she's always refused any offer his father made?'

'Well, Ryan's always been on the right side of Mrs Craven, as I said before,' remarked Maria. 'I for one wouldn't like to be around when D.J. gets wind of this. Unless he's in on the deal, too.'

'No. I'm pretty sure he knows nothing about it.' Liv let the end of the blueprint go, and as it sprang back into its cylindrical roll she half wished she hadn't stumbled on anything to do with it.

CHAPTER SIX

WHEN the children awoke they all went ashore to gather firewood for the barbecue Ryan had suggested they have on the beach that night. By the time they had enough dry branches, leaves and driftwood piled up the fishermen appeared around the headland and their expedition had obviously been successful. Roko held up a string of nice-sized snapper and they set about preparing the fire to cook them.

Liv's eyes searched Ryan's face, a dull flush creeping into her cheeks as his blue eyes mirrored her recollections of their lovemaking on the deck earlier in the afternoon, but a cold hardness was transposed upon that one burning moment before he turned from her and set about building the fire in a slight indentation they had made in the sand. A thousand questions trembled on her lips, questions about his intention to remain permanently in the area, questions about his association with the plans to develop Craven Island, questions . . . But she voiced none of them, curbing her curiosity.

The fish were delicious and they sat back replete as the russet sun slid down across the water and over the horizon, leaving a trail of colour highlighting the ripples of the waves and the edges of a few clouds that hung low in the sky.

Mike added more wood to the fire and they sat companionably about its bright warmth. Roko went back to the boat for his guitar and they all joined in a singalong until the children's eyelids began to droop and Liv and Maria decided to take them to bed. Both Melly and Sophy were already asleep.

'Come back when you've settled the kids, love,' said Mike, stretching out on the still warm sand as Maria carried little Sophy towards the jetty.

Liv went to struggle to her feet with the sleeping Melly and a dark shadow loomed over them.

'I'll carry her,' said Ryan, his hands going under the child's limp form and he lifted her effortlessly out of Liv's arms. 'Is Luke awake enough to walk?'

'Yes. Come on, Luke.' Liv put an arm around his shoulders to guide him, taking hold of Dino with her other hand.

Ryan waited while Liv turned down the bedclothes on one of the twin berths and then carefully lowered Melly into bed. He pulled the rugs up over her, tucking her in, pausing for a split second before he turned back to Liv as she went to turn down the other bed for Luke.

'Luke can have the upper bunk out here in the alcove. There's no need for you to squeeze in with Melly—I told you that,' he said softly, turning Luke's dragging footsteps out into the alcove where he swung him up into the top bunk and helped him settle under the rugs. 'There's a ladder here at the end of the bed if you want to get down in the night. I'll leave the light on in the passage. See you in the morning, son.' Ryan patted his shoulder and Luke nodded sleepily.

''Night, Luke.' A small pain began somewhere about Liv's heart and she turned sharply towards the main cabin with Ryan's soft footfalls right behind her.

'I think I'll stay here on board,' she said as Maria

joined them in the cabin, 'in case the children get out of bed.'

'They're dead to the world,' said Ryan.

'Well, I wouldn't want them to wander out and fall overboard,' she said, not wanting to return to the romantic beach bathed in afterglow, especially with Ryan, evoking memories . . .

'No,' Maria shuddered. 'I'll stay here with you, Liv.'

Ryan looked at them both and nodded. 'Okay. As you like. I'll douse the fire and we'll all come back on board and sit out on deck.'

'There's no need for you all to do that,' Maria began.

'Now, what fun would it be around a romantic fire without our womenfolk?' he grinned at Maria, his eyes resting momentarily on Liv before he turned and disappeared along the jetty.

It was quite late when they eventually retired. They all seemed loath to bring the evening to an end. The cool tangy breeze, the gentle rise and fall of the boat beneath them, Roko's pleasant singing and the romantic strumming of the guitar brought a sense of unreality, of languor, to this island paradise sitting in an empty ocean.

Catching an eloquent look that passed between Maria and Mike, Liv felt she could almost envy them their happiness in each other. Maria's head rested against Mike's shoulder, her arm lying along his thigh, her fingers gently moving over his knee.

Liv sat alone, telling herself firmly this was how she wanted it. She had waited tensely for Ryan to make a move to sit beside her and she also told herself she would move away if he did. But he didn't. He chose to sit alone as she was.

From where she sat she could see him out of the corner of her eye as he lounged back against part of the cabin structure, one leg bent, his arm resting on his raised knee. As he watched Roko strumming his guitar so Liv surreptitiously watched him.

He had an almost classical profile, straight nose, clearly defined sensual lips and firm chin. The soft breeze played with the inevitable lock of dark hair that fell over his brow. Just this secretive scrutiny could cause her senses to over-react. Her heartbeats raced, her breathing became constricted and she knew a deep yearning for what might have been. She had always been physically attracted to him, but eight years ago it had been the adoration of an adolescent. Now, she knew her responses went deeper, were more mature and the strength of the attraction she felt for him filled her with a fear. A fear of him and an even greater fear of herself.

Yes, the naïve and impressionable teenager she had been was no more. She was older now, more worldly, and she knew the pain and heartache Ryan could bring her. She had promised herself she would never allow him to get close enough to hurt her again and she fought the feelings rising within her. She would keep herself under tight control. If Ryan thought he could get to her as easily as he had eight years ago then it was up to her to prove that he couldn't be more mistaken.

And what about that episode on the upper deck just a few hours earlier? asked a little voice. Her heartbeats skipped. She could hardly be blamed for that, she told herself. He had taken her unawares. She had been asleep and therefore vulnerable. There would be no encore; she'd see he didn't get that close ever again.

Lying in the soft cosiness of her bunk, Liv still found her mind refusing to allow her the oblivion of sleep. Her body ached with tiredness while her thoughts still flitted about without respect for her fatigue.

The blueprint she had accidentally discovered that afternoon seemed to taunt her. Could Ryan possibly be the new owner of the island? It seemed incredible, but his name had unmistakably been on the bottom of the sheet. More importantly, how could he even contemplate doing such a thing to his father?

Ryan knew as well as anyone how fanatical D.J. had become over Craven Island, and now, to have his own son snap up the property under his very nose would be a huge blow to him. That Ryan was doing that very thing to get back on D.J. did cross Liv's mind, but she disregarded that idea, knowing Ryan would not be spiteful. He wouldn't plot and plan and wait his moment for revenge. Or would he?

However, his purchase of Craven Island for whatever reasons could only serve to widen further the gulf between father and son. Over the years that rift had gradually gaped until the whole world had caved in on them eight years ago.

Liv had known right from the beginning that Ryan's father was not pleased about his association with her. Not that he had anything against her personally; he was simply against her youth, and her presence was not in his plan of things for his elder son. Marriage for Ryan was to be at a later date to the daughter of one of his contemporaries, a girl who had poise and the years to take her place at Ryan's side, who could cope with his position in the community.

The seventeen-year-old daughter of a fisherman, especially a fisherman who stood up to D.J. at council meetings, was not even conceivable. And her own father had felt the same about Ryan, for similar reasons. Anyone born with a silver spoon in his mouth was not to be trusted, and when that person was the daredevil son of D. J. Denison, enough was said.

The day after Liv had met Ryan and Joel at the party, after the Denison brothers had dropped her home, the phone rang and Liv went to answer it with no premonition about who was on the other end of the line. Ryan's deep voice had rendered her speechless.

He had to go to Mackay on business and he wondered if she would care to come along for the drive. Could she be ready in half an hour?

In her mind Liv was again that young girl of seventeen, hurriedly donning a pair of blue denim jeans and a colourful overblouse, running a tidying brush through her fair hair, scribbling a hurried sketchily detailed note for her father and spending the remaining fifteen minutes in an agony of waiting, wondering if she should race out to Ryan's car when he pulled up or wait sedately for his knock on the door. Those minutes had dragged by with feverish slowness.

He drew up in front of their house and he had obviously collected his car from the repair shop. It was a rakish-looking racer, a bright red E-type Jaguar, with gleaming duco and chrome spoke wheels, its black soft top folded down so that the occupants could feel the wind in their hair, the sun on their faces.

Liv opened the door as he strode purposefully down the path and at the sight of her his charming smile lit his tanned face. He also wore jeans, the dark material worn a shade lighter where it hugged the firm strength of his thighs, and a pale blue sweat shirt, the colour a few shades lighter than the burning blue of his eyes, the shirt hanging loosely from his broad shoulders.

It had been a wonderful day. Whatever business Ryan had in Mackay he had transacted in no time and they spent the remainder of the afternoon driving and talking. They ate hamburgers and drank cans of Coke overlooking a deserted sweep of coastline, and all too soon they were home.

Of course he had drawn her lightly into his arms and kissed her, and Liv could still recall the rapture of that moment. Ryan had taught her that the kisses she had exchanged with the few boys of her own age she had been out with had been inefficacious things. His undeniable experience had guided her and her responsive young body had followed his lead. In all honesty her response had taken her by surprise and she had jumped hastily from the car, thanking him breathlessly for taking her with him, and his mouth had lifted in a slightly rueful and yet smug smile and he had raised one hand and roared away.

Agonisingly she had thought she wouldn't see him again, angry with herself for her gauche innocence. How he must have laughed at her inexperience, she tortured herself.

However, a few days later, as she walked down the main street in the village, the red Jaguar pulled into the kerb beside her. Ryan leant across and swung open the door and he hadn't needed to voice the invitation for her to slide into the passenger seat.

It was a few weeks before her father discovered that she was seeing Ryan Denison. Not that Liv had intentionally kept it from him; he had simply been working when Ryan called for her. And when he did find out Liv and her father had had what amounted to their first quarrel. Her father had loudly numbered Ryan's faults. Ryan Denison was far too old for her. He was reckless. He was irresponsible. He could only be amusing himself with her—and much more. That all these thoughts had occurred to Liv only served to fan her anger.

After that she had taken to arranging to meet Ryan away from the house and if he noticed he made no mention of it. Their lovemaking had grown more intense as the weeks passed, and one particular evening brought their relationship to a head.

On that evening they had shared a romantic and leisurely meal at a restaurant and on the way home Ryan parked the car off the road around the bay from the bungalow. Liv's all but illicit meetings with Ryan weighed heavily on her conscience and she returned his kisses with desperate fervour, trying to banish those guilt-laden disquietening thoughts from her mind.

Ryan's kisses hardened, became more potently possessive, and his hands moved under her loose blouse to unclip her bra. The torrential tide of pure emotion his caresses evoked clutched her young body, shocking her into almost rigidity, and instead of moving away Ryan pulled her close, drawing her against him so that she could feel the tremor of his own arousal and she suddenly became aware of how easily she could allow herself to submit completely, and this realisation filled her with fear and she pushed against him with all her strength.

For one terrible moment she thought he would fight back, use his superior strength to subdue her, but he let her go with just as jarring suddenness and sat back in his seat, his breathing ragged, his hands clasping the steering wheel. Liv crouched in her own seat feeling more wretched, more despairing than she had ever felt in her young life.

'Ryan?' she appealed to him at last. 'I'm sorry.' Her whispering voice broke.

He turned back to her then, his face pale in the moonlight, and he took her hand in his. 'No, it's I who should be apologising,' he sighed. 'I'm sorry I frightened you. I'm afraid I got a bit carried away and for a moment I forgot how young and—well——' he released her hand and flicked on the ignition, 'I think I'd better take you home.'

She didn't hear from him for a week and she lost count of the number of times she lifted the phone to call him, only to replace the receiver, tears streaming down her cheeks. When he called to invite her to a party a friend of his was having she all but wept with relief, and later, if she realised he was ensuring they spent little time alone, she was only too gratified to be with him under any conditions.

The gilt-edged invitation arrived the next week. D. J. Denison requested the pleasure of the company of Mr Charles Jansen and his daughter, Olivia, at the

Coming of Age of his younger son, Joel, etc. Her father had read the card slowly and thrown it carelessly on the table.

'Send our inability to accept,' he said firmly.

'Oh, but Dad, couldn't we go, please?' Liv pleaded. 'Joel's such a nice person. It would be rude to refuse to go to his party.'

'I thought I told you to keep away from the Denisons. They're not for you,' he said grimly.

'All your friends will be there. The Kingstons are going, and the Williams,' she told him.

Her father mumbled irritably. 'Well, maybe I should put in an appearance, keep old D.J. on his toes, the old reprobate.' He glanced at Liv. 'All right, we'll go. But I'll be there to see you don't go pairing off with Ryan Denison!'

As the evening of the party drew near Liv was almost sick with excitement. She had bought a new dress, a very daring dress, which left her shoulders bare and swirled in soft folds about her legs as she walked. Her hand shook as she carefully applied her make-up and her fair shoulder-length hair shone like a shimmering halo around her head.

Her father, a trifle ill at ease in his good suit, frowned at the tanned expanse of bare skin she was exposing, but she hurried him out to the car before he could even attempt to send her in to change.

It was the first time Liv had driven up the private road to the Denison home and as the road wound through the trees and the house came into view she caught her breath in wonderment. All alight for the party, the house looked like a huge floating mansion, an illusion conjured up by a daydreaming imagination. Her exclamation of pleasure had been met with ill grace by her father.

'Humph! That's the Denisons for you. Always the exhibitionists. Big house, big money—and always plenty of say.'

Thomas, the butler, had opened the door to them and led them inside to where Joel was receiving his guests. Catching sight of them, he hurried forward, his face smiling welcome.

'Good evening, Mr Jansen—Liv. Thanks for coming along.'

'Thank you for inviting us, and happy birthday.' Liv proffered her gift.

'Don't I get a kiss from the best looking girl in the district?' he asked as Liv's father moved on to speak to D.J.

Liv laughed and, putting her hands on his shoulders, kissed him quickly on the cheek.

'Just because you've reached the ripe old age of twenty-one it doesn't give you licence to go about kissing every girl within cooee, little brother,' Ryan's hand folded around Liv's as he stood beside her, 'especially this particular girl.' His eyes moved over her.

Liv's legs had turned to water and she let her own eyes drink in his handsomeness. In a light blue safari suit with a contrasting dark blue shirt he looked big and safe and he quite literally took her breath away.

'How are you, Mr Jansen?' Ryan offered the older man his hand as Liv's father rejoined them and reluctantly shook hands with Ryan.

Then some more guests arrived and they had to move on, Mr Jansen joining the group of men where D.J. was holding centre stage while Liv walked across to a huddle of young people most of whom were known to her.

To her disappointment Ryan didn't seek her out as she had expected he would and the evening began to lose some of its appeal. However, as they made to file in to supper he materialised beside her, his arm going lightly about her waist.

'Did I tell you you look absolutely ravishing tonight, Miss Jansen?' he said softly, his breath teasing her ear, and she turned adoring eyes on him. 'Look at me like that for much longer and I'll spirit you away to some secluded spot where we have no audience, Blue Eyes.'

The supper was lavish and delicious and the wine plentiful. Sitting alongside Liv, Ryan kept their glasses topped up and she soon began to feel just a little lightheaded. To have him seated beside her was an intoxication in itself.

They toasted Joel's health and speeches were made before the party split into age groups again, the young people retiring to the huge rumpus room to dance and the older guests sitting chatting in the living room.

Ryan had discarded his jacket and loosened a couple of buttons on his shirt as they danced and his eyes, seemingly brighter, more intense in their scrutiny, set Liv's body aflame. With deft precise movements he manoeuvred them to the outskirts of the dancers and before she knew what he had in mind he had swung her out into the empty hallway. Pulling her close into his arms, he kissed her desperately.

'I've been wanting to do that all evening,' he said huskily, and as he went to kiss her again a couple of people moved out of the rumpus room, laughing and teasing when they noticed Liv still held in the circle of Ryan's arms. He bore their banter with smiling good humour and when they were alone again he took Liv's hand and led her down the hallway and out on to a dimly lit covered courtyard.

'Where are we going?' Liv whispered, her fingers curled within his, the cool air causing her to stumble a little dizzily.

'Where we won't be disturbed,' he chuckled, and they picked their way down the moonlit steps to the beach below.

'Take off your shoes,' he said, and Liv kicked off her high-heeled sandals and watched Ryan, now barefoot, roll up the bottoms of his expensive slacks without a moment's concern about them getting crushed or stained.

Hand in hand they jumped down the remaining steps, luxuriating in the sensation of the warm fine sand between their toes. Like children they raced laughing across the beach, the sound of music and laughter fading into the darkness behind them.

'Ryan, stop! I can't run any farther.' Liv stopped and clutched her side. 'I think I must have eaten too much!'

Ryan undid the remaining buttons on his shirt and pulled it free of his trousers, letting the breeze cool his warm skin. 'I didn't realise it was so hot inside. Phew! What we need now is a swim to cool off.' His eyes gleamed like black coals. 'How about it, Liv?'

She laughed a little breathlessly. 'I didn't bring my suit.'

'Neither did I,' he chuckled softly, 'so I guess that leaves our birthday suits. Are you game?'

'No, I . . . I couldn't,' Liv protested weakly.

'Come on. No one's here to see us.' His white teeth flashed in the moonlight as he smiled down at her. 'I dare you, Liv.'

'You shouldn't—well, you shouldn't go swimming when you've been drinking, Ryan,' Liv said quickly as he shrugged his arms out of his shirt, letting it fall to the sand. 'You might get a cramp and drown.'

'Are you trying to tell me I'm drunk, Liv Jansen? I assure you I'm just pleasantly inebriated.' He unbuckled his belt. 'You'd better come in with me to see that I don't drown, hadn't you?' His slacks slid over his narrow hips. 'Leave your underlcothes on if you're modest.'

'I'm . . . I'm only wearing bikini pants,' Liv stammered, the darkness hiding the deep blush that surged over her face as she kept her eyes fixed on his chin.

'Then wear them.' He hooked one finger in the elasticized top of her dress. 'Need a hand with any zippers?'

'N . . . N . . . No.'

'Okay,' he chuckled again. 'See you in the surf.' He turned and slipped out of his brief shorts and ran down to the water's edge, the moonlight playing over his muscular back.

Liv stood transfixed, undecided. Suppose he did drown out there? Standing here trembling she wouldn't even know he had slipped under the waves until it was far too late. Perhaps she should go in. She turned back to the house, the lights glowing in the distance. No one was on the beach except the two of them, so there would be no one to see them.

With sudden recklessness, before she allowed herself time to change her mind, Liv pulled her dress over her head and stepped out of her panties. A mixture of emancipated excitement and horror at her wanton behaviour warred inside her as she ran down to the water and immersed herself in its salty chilliness. The first touch of that coolness made her gasp, but she was soon revelling in the feeling of freedom, of being alone in the silky moonlit sea.

But she shouldn't be alone. Ryan should be here. Her eyes searched the surface of the water, panic rising within her. Where was he? His name trembled on her lips as strong arms wrapped around her, lifting her bodily upwards, only to let her fall ignobly back into the water. When she surfaced, gasping for breath and wiping strands of wet hair from her face, he was standing nearby in water a little above his waist.

Liv made a retaliating dive for him, but he slipped easily to the side, reappearing to up-end her again. However, this time she was ready for him and wrapped her arms around him, pulling him with her into the water. They surfaced together laughing and gasping, her arms still on his shoulders, his hands still resting on her waist.

The moon seemed to glow brighter at that moment and Ryan's eyes moved down over her glistening body. They became still, their laughter dying on their lips. Involuntarily his hands moved from her waist to cup each breast and her breasts swelled, the nipples hardening as the spark of mutually awakening desire surged as easily to the surface as their bodies had done only moments earlier through the oily sea.

They leant together, his hands covering her breasts, his lips nibbling sensuously on hers, his hardening maleness kindling a throbbing necessity for fulfilment that rose to engulf her. His arms slid to encircle her, their damp bodies straining together in impetuous arousal.

Ryan swung her lightly into his arms, moving through the surf on to the beach, stopping when the water lapped his ankles to claim her lips once more and he let her body slide sensually down the length of his. Their kisses became more intense, more all-consuming, and they sank on to the sand with the ebb and flow of two or three inches of foam insinuating itself about them.

All thought of resistance, of denial, left her as Ryan's body covered hers. She wanted this desperate closeness as much as he did. If the thought crossed her mind that what they were doing was wrong she cast that thought aside, telling herself she loved Ryan, always had and always would love him and that there could never be anyone else but him.

Afterwards he held her tightly to him, wiping the tears from her cheeks. 'I hurt you—Liv, I'm sorry,' he said huskily. 'I couldn't make the first time any easier.'

She shook her head. 'It's all right. I . . . I love you, Ryan.' She touched his face with her hand, her heart in the eyes she turned up to him.

He looked down at her moonkissed face for immeasurable seconds, his expression in the shadow inscrutable, before he pulled her to her feet and they walked in silence up to where they had left their clothes.

What could be wrong? Had she failed him in some way? Embarrassed him? She swallowed a sob and he turned back to look at her.

'Liv, please. Don't cry,' he said huskily. 'You couldn't despise me more than I despise myself at this moment, believe me.'

'I . . . I don't despise you, Ryan,' she said shakily. 'It wasn't your fault.'

He ran his fingers distractedly through his wet hair. 'I shouldn't have lost control. I must have been drunker than I thought I was.'

Liv flinched at his words. Did he mean, if he'd been sober he wouldn't have wanted her? 'Didn't . . . didn't it mean anything to you?' she whispered, and went to turn away from him, but his hands reached out to swing her back, his fingers biting into the flesh of her arms. At the touch of her skin his punishing grip relaxed, sliding over the smoothness of her shoulders to cup her face.

'Of course it meant something to me,' he said gruffly, drawing her back against him, 'but I shouldn't have let it happen. I should have had more self-restraint. God, Liv, you're so young,' he muttered, his lips moving against her temple down to her earlobe, and she felt the renewed tenseness in his body. 'We should get dressed,' he said softly, making no move to do so, 'but all of a sudden that's not what I have in mind to do.'

This time their lovemaking was less fervent, more mutually merging, with Ryan teaching and Liv the willing pupil, and their oneness carried them to an ecstatic fulfilment. Afterwards, content, they slept in each other's arms, lying on the smooth sand, oblivious of the passage of time, not hearing the calls, not seeing the forms approaching, unaware of the encroachments on their domain, into their love-sated world, until a torchlight lit their bodies and was jerked away and the voices abruptly ceased.

Ryan came instantly awake, springing to his feet, dragging Liv with him as she struggled to banish the muzziness of sleep that clung to her and then blinked in horror at the two rigid forms standing in the pool of light from the lowered torch. Standing calmly, shielding her body with his own until Liv had dragged her dress over her head, Ryan made no comment. He simply waited and then reached down for his trousers and unhurriedly pulled them over his hips.

'Have you found them?' Liv's father's voice floated across the sound of the waves as he hurried up to join the other two figures.

'Yes, they're here.' D.J.'s voice sounded controlled, but when he looked back at his elder son it filled with contempt. 'You've gone too far this time, Ryan,' he said, almost shaking with suppressed anger. 'That a son of mine could . . .'

'Liv, are you all right?' Joel moved towards her.

'Yes, of course I'm all right,' she said, suddenly filled with shame. Her whole body suffused with colour and what had seemed so beautiful, so right, before, now began to appear degrading and sordid. 'We . . . we fell asleep,' she said defensively.

'What the hell's been going on here?' Charles Jansen's voice was ragged from his jog along the beach. 'We've been worried sick about you, Liv. We found your shoes back on the steps.' His eyes took in her wet hair. 'Liv? Have you been swimming?'

'Let's get back to the house,' said Ryan flatly. 'There's no point in standing out here all night.'

'Liv, what's been going on?' persisted her father.

'We'll talk back at the house, Jansen,' remarked D.J. as they turned to walk in an uneasy silence back along the beach. 'Thank God everyone's gone home.'

CHAPTER SEVEN

LYING in her bunk on Ryan's yacht, Liv cringed inwardly as flashes of remembrance, vivid visions of the scene that followed, came back to taunt her. Her arms moved to wrap themselves about her body to offer some form of protection from the remembered agony.

Her father had been momentarily stunned into silence when the whole thing was made clear to him, and then he and D.J. had yelled accusations loudly, while Ryan stood to one side not saying anything, his face the expressionless mask of a stranger.

When Liv's control finally broke, when she was no longer able to bear the arguments, it was Joel who had put his arms around her, comforted her, and wiped away the tears that were coursing down her cheeks. As her sobs subsided she had looked up into Joel's sympathetic eyes, his face mirroring some of her wretchedness and something else she found hard to define—pain, disappointment. And she looked away, feeling humiliated and cheap.

She had calmed down a little in his arms, and her next recollections had been of her father's demand that Ryan marry her and right away. Only when marriage was mentioned did Ryan attempt to enter the conversation, and his words struck ice in Liv's veins. He wasn't ready for marriage, he said. There were things he had to do before he took on the responsibilities of marriage.

Liv's father turned on him then, looked ready to physically attack him, his face suffused with an unhealthy colour as his anger threatened to get the upper hand. But D.J.'s voice overrode them all. Ryan would marry Liv, face his responsibilities for once, and then he could get out of the house, out of the state, out of the country for all his father cared, and he could take only what he could carry. There would be no financial help. But he would marry Liv—and that was final.

Liv's eyes moved back to Ryan as he faced his father, his jaw set and angry, his eyes warring with his father's. But the unkindest cut of all was the way Ryan's stormy blue eyes had slid away from Liv's imploring gaze.

Their marriage was a quiet one, the total opposite to any usual function associated with the Denisons, and an hour after the ceremony Ryan had left. Liv hadn't seen him alone after those now almost dreamlike moments on the beach. He hadn't even kissed her during the ceremony. And when their hands had touched as Ryan slipped the ring on her finger they had both drawn away as through they were burned.

She hadn't seen him until he had materialised out of the darkness three weeks ago. In fact she hadn't heard any word of him until the twins were almost two years old, when she had been advised by the bank that he had arranged for an allowance to be paid into her account each month. In all those years she hadn't touched a cent of it. She had wanted nothing from him.

As she turned on her side, feeling the dampness of tears trickle on to her pillow, a wave of self-pity swept over her. No. She had wanted nothing from him. Not ever. But he had given her a most precious gift—her beautiful children. And she couldn't imagine her life without them. Although in the beginning she had felt nothing for the life that was growing within her.

After Ryan's departure Liv had simply turned quietly into herself, not leaving the bungalow, sitting for hours on the patio gazing out to sea, or walking alone along the beach, shutting out anyone who made any overtures towards her. Her father. Joel. She had erected an imaginary glass cage about herself, touching no one and letting no one touch her.

The fact that she could be pregnant had not registered on her de-activated thought processes, and only when her father noticed how sick she had been on a number of mornings and arranged for a doctor to call was her condition discovered. She had taken the news without any sign of emotion. She had not wanted the child, nor had she *not* wanted it.

Her father had been almost beside himself with anxiety, but it was Joel who had taken things into his own hands. He sat with Liv and talked to her for hours, talked long and harshly, until some of his barbs had chipped away and pierced her defences, his words seeping into her consciousness. He called her selfish and thoughtless and a thousand other unflattering things until she had eventually turned on him, shouting out her self-pity.

How could he know how she felt? How much she

had suffered? No one could know, she cried out in anger. And Joel had goaded her again until she began to cry for the first time since the night of the party. He held her until she was all cried out and then he had set about picking up the pieces and putting her back together again. He talked some more—about the baby, about her future, and about the baby's future. Until she became aware of the tiny life within her, began to realise just what it meant. All the love that she had given Ryan which he had handed so callously back to her she had turned on the unborn child and gradually she had regained her equilibrium, brought everything back into perspective. Yes, Joel had been her salvation and only she knew how much he had done to save her sanity. Because she had been on the brink of teetering over and he had brought her down on the right side. It would have been so easy to fall in love with Joel over the years, but they were both aware of another face between them.

Eventually Liv drifted off to sleep, only to be disturbed from her fitful dozing by a hand gently touching her shoulder. She rolled over, blinking in the semi-darkness, aware of some noise she couldn't place. The reading light over her bunk had been switched on and dimmed, but it was bright enough for her to recognise the owner of the hand that had awoken her as he leant over her.

'What's the matter? What are you doing here?' She clutched the bedclothes up under her arms protectively.

'I'm afraid I'll have to share your bunk. Roko's stretched out on the divan in the main cabin,' Ryan said evenly, his hand on the bedclothes, 'and I don't fancy sleeping on the floor when I can be more than comfortable here.'

'You must be mad if you think I'm going to let you . . .'

'Keep your voice down, unless you want to wake everyone on board,' he said tightly.

'You are not getting in this bed!' Liv whispered urgently.

His eyes locked with hers.

'What's so suddenly wrong with the open air and the stars above?' she asked sarcastically, while her heart beat an agitated tattoo.

'If you'd stop talking long enough to listen you'd realise it's raining. A tropical shower,' he said drily, and she saw that his hair was ruffled and damp and looked as though he had rubbed it partially dry.

And now she could place the sound, the patter of rain on the deck above. Her eyes dropped lower over his smooth torso, her mouth suddenly dry. His only clothing was a pair of very brief underpants, and her body tensed warily. 'What about Alesi?'

'She's sound asleep in her bunk below Luke's. She came down before the shower started. Now, move over. I'm tired and I want to get some sleep.' He pulled back the rugs and slid on to the bunk beside her.

What had previously seemed like a comfortably large bed now diminished to cramped narrowness as Liv flattened herself against the cabin wall, her body stiff and tension-filled. Ryan reached up to switch off the light and turned on his side, his back to her. Liv lay still, her eyes wide open.

Ryan sighed deeply. 'For God's sake, relax,' he breathed into the darkness.

His voice only made her press closer to the wall.

'Liv,' he rolled slightly over towards her, 'as you told me very opportunely once before, Melly's in the next bed. Besides, I didn't have to use force the last time we made love, and if I wanted you now we both know I still wouldn't have to force you—so go to sleep, and be thankful I'm not in the mood.' He turned back and was soon breathing evenly.

Gradually Liv forced the tension from her flexed muscles and surprisingly she slept. At some time during the night she turned towards Ryan and he drew her arm around him as she moulded herself into the curve of his back.

When her eyelids fluttered open daylight was streaming into the cabin through the uncovered porthole over the bunk where Melly lay still sleeping. Recollection flooded her mind and her eyes flew to the place where Ryan had lain, but she was alone. Could she have dreamed the whole thing? But no. There was the indentation of his head in the pillow.

She sat up and peered through her own porthole at the clear blue sky. The overnight rain had cleared, leaving the island looking fresh and sparkling.

There was a soft tap on the open cabin door and Ryan stepped inside with Luke close on his heels. They each carried two mugs of tea and when Luke had set his and Melly's on the table between the beds he hopped up beside his sister, who was rubbing her sleepy eyes.

Wordlessly Ryan handed Liv a mug of tea and sat down on the end of her bunk. 'Seems as though the rain's gone,' he said, raising his steaming mug to his lips, his eyes moving over Liv's flushed face.

'Ah, so this is where everyone is,' remarked Alesi, stepping into the cabin and sinking on to the bunk with the twins. 'You're a sleepyhead, Liv. Ryan and I have already been swimming.' Her smile was directed at Ryan and he smiled back.

'I'm afraid I had a restless night,' said Liv, fixing her eyes on her tea.

'Oh. That's not good. I suppose you're not used to the movements of the boat,' suggested the other girl. 'Me, I was born in a boat, so I found my sea legs very early.'

'You didn't have a bad dream, did you, Mummy?' asked Melly, peering around Luke.

Liv's eyes went to Ryan and he grinned mockingly. 'Something like that,' she said sweetly, turning to smile at her daughter.

'Well, come on, Luke. We'll go toss the line over the side, see if we can hook a butter bream or a trevally for breakfast.' Ryan stood up and Luke jumped eagerly off the bed.

'Can I come, too?' asked Melly.

'You're not dressed,' said Luke dismissingly.

'I can get dressed really quickly,' said his sister, unbuttoning the top of her pyjamas.

'Come up when you're ready, Melly,' said Ryan as he disappeared into the hallway followed by Luke and Alesi.

Liv climbed out of bed and helped Melly dress, her mind on the Fijian girl, and as Melly ran after the others Liv sank down on to her bunk. That Alesi was infatuated with Ryan was obvious. Her eyes followed him, her smile was directed only at him. She was so transparent. Just the way she Liv used to be! Could

Ryan and Alesi be having an affair? Then why had Ryan told her he wanted her and the twins with him? Maybe he wanted to have his cake and to eat it, too.

A spurt of jealousy stirred her into jumping off the bunk and collecting her clothes, her mind filled with despair. She turned to the bed where they had lain and had to fight the desire to put her head to the hollow in the pillow where Ryan's head had left a visible imprint.

What a blind fool she was! She loved him as much now as she had ever done, maybe more so, because now he was a man and not the rosy image she had created all those years ago. That image had faded away and now she recognised the person he was, with human faults, and could love him in spite of them. That he was still ruthless as far as getting what he wanted she didn't doubt, and if he was to discover how she felt about him he would surely take advantage of it and her. At all costs he mustn't guess. She must keep him at a distance, make sure she was never alone with him.

'Hey, Mum! Breakfast's ready,' called Luke from the galley. 'We've caught some fish. Even Melly caught one,' he told her excitedly.

Breakfast was a jovial meal and if Liv had little to say the fact wasn't noticed or commented upon. They all sat around the table in the main cabin with the children sitting separately at a breakfast bench.

'I thought I heard it raining last night,' remarked Maria. 'Anyone else notice, or was I hearing things?'

'Rained cats and dogs for a while,' replied Roko. 'Ryan and I had to run for it. We got saturated. I stretched out here in the cabin. Where did you get to, Ryan?'

'Oh, I found a cosy spot,' he grinned, and the others laughed, although Maria and Alesi gave Liv's flushed face rather piercing looks, even if they were for different reasons.

Liv and Maria lay sunbathing on the beach as they watched the children playing in the shallows.

'Mike says Ryan has bought Craven Island,' said Maria. 'They were talking about it yesterday and Mike says Ryan has some fantastic plans for the island, really great ideas that are going to make it a roaring success. And it will create so many jobs for the local people.'

'I've no doubt it will be a success if Ryan has anything to do with it.' Liv couldn't keep the bitterness out of her voice and Maria looked at her sharply. 'I'm sorry, Maria,' Liv sighed. 'I shouldn't take it out on you. I just can't not be antagonistic towards him. Just the mention of his name and I'm on the defensive.'

'Perhaps you've conditioned yourself to think like that, Liv, because he hurt you,' said Maria quietly.

Liv shook her head, unwilling to even consider that there may have been some truth in Maria's words. And her father's attitude hadn't helped. Right up till his death he had never had a good word to say about Ryan, and D.J. never spoke of his elder son. It was only to the children that Liv had ever moderated herself about him, trying for their sakes not to colour their outlook on the father they had never known.

Which brought her back to the main problem— telling the twins about Ryan. 'I'll have to tell the twins soon,' she absently spoke her words out loud to Maria.

'Why not do it while Ryan's with you? Then you could both talk to them. And after all, the responsibility shouldn't just rest with you,' Maria said logically.

'I don't know if I could remain cool,' Liv frowned as Ryan came walking along the jetty from the yacht.

Liv watched him as he strode purposefully towards them, moving with an unconscious lithe animal grace. His muscles were firm and highly tuned and he had about him an air of success and absolute self-confidence. No one could be immune to the attraction he emitted, certainly not Liv, and she felt her anger rise to colour her cheeks. That her anger was directed at her own traitorous body didn't make it any easier to quell.

'We'll have to head back earlier than I'd intended,' he said, stretching out on the sand beside Liv. 'I don't like the look of those cumulo-nimbus clouds gathering out there, and according to the weather report the seas will be getting choppy in the late afternoon. So rather than have everyone uncomfortable we might push off in a half hour or so, when the others come in from the reef. Pity to cut the day short,' he finished, his eyes on the offending cloud patterns.

And as much as Liv had wanted this trip to be over, with Craven Island growing smaller, she experienced an unprecedented twinge of regret that they were leaving.

They were back at the wharf at Shute Harbour before the swells were more than moderate and Liv went below to collect their gear, stacking it on deck ready to go ashore with the Costellos.

'I'll drive you home, Liv,' said Ryan as he passed her on his way aft to take the wheel.

'I came with Mike and Maria,' she said quietly. 'They can take me home.'

He stopped and turned on her, his eyes stormily telling her he'd like to shake her. 'I'm taking you home,' he said evenly. 'I have something to discuss with you.' And he continued on his way.

By the time Ryan and Roko had checked and stowed away the sails it was growing late. The Costellos had gone and Liv sat lost in her own thoughts waiting for Ryan to finish and drive them home. He didn't seem to be in any hurry, and she seethed inwardly. The twins were quite happy with the arrangement and were amusing themselves trying to catch the colourful little fish swimming in the blue waters around the jetty posts, and they were reluctant to put the fishing gear away when Ryan was finally ready to leave. Alesi and Roko left at the same time to visit friends.

Liv unlocked the bungalow door and the twins raced through to the back door and down to the beach. Walking down the hallway, Liv deposited their bags in her room and, nerves tensed, followed Ryan out on to the back patio where he stood with his hands in the pockets of his faded denim jeans watching Luke and Melly running about on the sand.

Liv in turn stood watching his broad back, wondering what he was thinking as he watched the twins, wondering if he had any regrets over missing seven of their most formative years. A lump rose in her throat and she swallowed determinedly. 'What did you want to talk to be about?' she asked brusquely.

For a moment she thought he hadn't heard her as he remained where he was, but eventually he turned. 'I want to ask you a favour,' he said seriously.

'What kind of a favour?' she asked, eyeing him warily.

'Let's go indoors,' he motioned for her to precede him inside.

They had just stepped into the kitchen when the front door bell pealed and with one glance at Ryan Liv left him to answer it, experiencing a sensation of momentary reprieve. However, this feeling was short-lived, for on the porch stood Martin Wilson.

'Good evening, Olivia. I hoped I'd catch you in.' He turned for a moment in the direction of Ryan's silver Mercedes parked in the driveway. 'I trust I haven't called at an inconvenient time.'

'Oh. Hello, Martin,' Liv's voice was a little breathless as she tried to think up an excuse to send him away before Ryan came out. 'I . . . We've just this minute arrived home and I . . .'

'Who is it, darling?' Ryan's voice came from behind her and Liv froze at the intimately affectionate tone he used.

Martin's eyes had narrowed as he gazed at the man standing behind Liv, and when Ryan's arm went familiarly around her waist his eyes turned to Liv in amazed disbelief. Liv's throat had closed on her speech and Ryan held out his other hand.

'How do you do? I'm Ryan Denison, Liv's husband.'

'Olivia, is this true?' Martin ignored the other man's outstretched hand and Ryan shrugged.

'Let's see, you must be Martin Wilson. Liv's told me about you.'

'She has?' Martin mouthed incredulously, looking back at Liv.

'Ryan, please.' Liv found her voice at last. 'Leave Martin and me alone for a minute.'

Ryan gave Martin a level look before shrugging again. 'I'll go and start dinner,' he said good-naturedly, and disappeared back to the kitchen.

'Olivia, what's going on?' Martin began. 'Is he your husband? I thought you said you never saw him.'

'Yes, he is, but I don't . . . Oh, Martin, it's not what you think,' said Liv hurriedly, and took a deep breath before continuing. 'I'm sorry, Martin. I meant to tell you when you rang, but . . .'

'Was it his boat you went sailing on?' he asked.

'Yes, but . . .'

'How long has he been back here?' Martin threw at her.

'About three weeks, but . . .'

'Three weeks!' Martin's fair skin turned mottled red. 'I see. Well, I'll leave you to it,' he said, his lip curling. 'I think I may have overestimated you, Olivia.' He turned to walk off.

'Martin, wait!' Liv put her hand on his arm.

He looked down at it, shrugged it off and walked away. Liv watched him go, knowing she shouldn't feel this suggestion of relief and because she did she felt guilty. Spinning on her heel, she marched into the kitchen, bent on giving Ryan a piece of her mind.

Melly was standing on a chair watching Ryan stirring something delicious-smelling in a cooking pot while Luke was happily setting the table, a task he usually hated doing.

'The men are preparing dinner tonight,' Luke told her.

Ryan's eyes met hers across the kitchen, his bland innocence goading her further, but she held her tongue, not wanting to upset the children.

'Dinner's nearly ready already,' said Melly, 'and it's all from tins.' Her eyes were large with wonderment before she turned back to Ryan. 'Are you sure it will taste all right?'

'Guaranteed to. I'm the king of the tin can gourmet world,' Ryan smiled at her. 'Now, if everyone will be seated we can partake of my "what you have" stew.'

The twins laughed, sitting at their places, while Ryan served up the meal. Liv sat quietly in her seat, feeling as though a bite of food would choke her, but it was surprisingly good.

'Wasn't that great, Mum?' Luke set his knife and fork on his empty plate. 'Now the girls have to do the dishes,' he grinned. 'That's the rules.'

'Fair enough,' said Liv, glancing at the kitchen clock, 'and then it's bath time and off to bed for you two. You've had a hectic weekend and there's school tomorrow.'

As she tucked the children into bed Ryan stood in the doorway bidding them goodnight, and Liv knew she should tell him how badly she thought he had treated Martin, but her anger seemed to have abated and she followed him into the living room feeling unsure of herself and him.

CHAPTER EIGHT

'About that favour, Liv.' Ryan stood by the window, eyes fixed out in the darkness.

'After the way you treated Martin you can have the audacity to ask me favours?' Liv asked incredulously. 'You can forget any favours, Ryan.'

'That insipid prig couldn't make you happy, Liv,' he said decisively. 'You'd be bored to death with him inside a month. Besides, I didn't tell him a thing that wasn't the truth.'

'It wasn't what you said but the way you said it—and I resent your interference in what's none of your business!' Liv stormed.

'You don't mean to tell me you were seriously considering marrying him?' he asked, his eyes holding hers.

It would have been so easy to say yes, but she knew inside herself that she could never have married Martin, even if Ryan hadn't returned. Ryan was right, he would have bored her to tears. Her eyes fell from his.

'I thought not,' he said confidently.

Liv sank into a lounge chair, suddenly weary of the whole conversation. 'Ryan, I'm tired. Just tell me whatever you want to tell me and then go,' she said flatly, half wishing she had remained standing, matching at least some of his intimidating height.

He didn't reply for a moment and she wondered if he could possibly be undecided about his choice of words. But she dismissed that idea as being totally out of character.

'I've bought Craven Island,' he said at last without preamble.

'I know,' she replied hesitantly.

He nodded. 'Mike told Maria and Maria told you.'

Liv shook her head and explained about finding the blueprint. 'I wouldn't have believed Mrs Craven would sell that island. How did you manage to talk her into it?'

He shrugged. 'I came along at the right time with the right amount of cash.'

Liv's eyes searched his face, forming a fleeting impression that his answer was not exactly the truth and wondering again how he had come by the wealth he seemed to have acquired.

Ryan smiled crookedly. 'It's all strictly legitimate,' he said, reading her thoughts. 'I've been fortunate enough to purchase the right merchandise cheaply and have it on hand at the peak of demand.' He walked about the small living room, from the window back to stare at a framed seascape hanging on the wall. 'One of yours?'

'Yes.'

'It's good.'

'Thank you. I do reasonably well with them.'

He nodded, turning back towards her. 'I'm having a dinner at the hotel in Airlie and I want you to be there, act as my hostess,' he said at last.

Liv looked up at him in disbelief. 'What kind of a dinner?'

'To launch my new project on Craven Island. I've invited everyone around the district who could be for or against the resort so that they'll know what's planned and we can deal with any protests before we start.' He moved back to the window.

'Some of the facilities I'm putting into the Craven Island resort are new innovations, and people don't care much on the whole for change,' he grimaced. 'I'm going to talk them into thinking the ideas are the best thing tourist-wise to hit the area in decades.'

'Even if they're all against it?'

'They won't be after the evening's over,' he said assuredly.

'And what does being a hostess involve?' Liv asked without expression, thinking he had the most self-confidence of anyone she had met, including his father.

'Just being by my side, looking as attractive as I know you can,' he smiled. 'Those I can't win with words I'll bedazzle on to my side.'

'And just why should I do this——' she paused, 'favour for you?'

His eyes mocked her. 'Maybe you could look on it as a means to an end. As soon as the resort gets under way I can be off out of your hair.'

The shock his words created hit her like a physical blow, but she managed to school her features before he turned back to her. 'I thought you were staying?' she said, wondering why the idea of his leaving had suddenly lost its appeal. But of course she knew why.

'Who knows?' he said enigmatically, and they looked at each other in silence.

'Ryan, why did you come back?' she heard herself ask. 'Was it to prove a point to D.J.? Because that's what he's going to think, what everyone's going to think.'

'I'm afraid I don't much care what everyone thinks, and the reason I came back had nothing to do with D.J.,' he said. 'Why should I want to prove anything to him after all this time? Perhaps in the beginning . . .' he shrugged. 'I gave up even thinking about D.J.'s opinion of me. He could never see my way on anything in the past. He stifled me, knowing all the while that I'd never be a "yes" man. How he'll feel about my plans for Craven Island now—well, who can say? But I intend discussing it with him before the dinner. And as for the island itself, D.J. could have matched the price I paid for it, but Mrs Craven chose to sell to me simply because she liked the ideas I set out to her.'

He leant nonchalantly against a large lounge chair. 'Apart from the island, I came back to try to make something of our marriage, which you seem loath to do. That decision seems to have been taken out of my hands,' he eyed her steadily. 'The ball's in your court there.'

'And as I told you before, I'm quite happy as I am,' she stated, hoping he didn't notice it was said with less conviction.

'That's your prerogative, but I'd still like to get to know the twins.'

Liv stood up angrily. 'How can you expect me to let you pick them up now that you've decided you want to? Tomorrow you may want to put them down again. No, Ryan, I don't think it's a good idea.'

'Are you afraid you may have to share them, Liv?' he asked grimly.

'That's a despicable thing to say!'

'No more so than what you just accused me of. But

do you think it's fair to deny me access to my children? Look, Liv, when I discovered that they existed I wasn't in any position to return financially or emotionally. At that time I would have done more harm than good, but things are different now. Can't we try to be civilised about it?'

'And I repeat, I don't want the children hurt. Just your presence here could do them irreparable damage. If someone chose to be nasty and told them . . .' Liv's voice faded away.

'Then we should tell them. And soon,' he said emphatically.

'I know, but . . .'

Ryan ran his hand through his hair. 'I have to go away for a few days, down to Brisbane. Come to dinner on the yacht on Friday night and we'll talk to them together where we won't be disturbed.'

Liv paused undecidedly.

'It has to be done, Liv. No matter how much you dislike the idea.'

'All right,' Liv sighed.

'I'll pick you up about six-thirty. And Liv, about that other matter,' he took his wallet out and extracted some notes, 'take this and buy yourself a dress for the occasion. Something slinky.'

'I have clothes, Ryan.' She ignored the money he held out.

'I know you have,' he said exasperatedly, and put the money on the coffee table, 'but just this once let me buy you the dress in appreciation of your helping me out on the night. Take Alesi with you if you like. She has good taste.' He glanced at his watch. 'I'll have to be off now. I've a business call coming through in twenty minutes.' He walked to the door. 'I'll see you on Friday,' he said, and let himself out of the front door.

After the sound of his car had disappeared into the distance Liv sat looking at the money lying on the coffee table, unable to bring herself to touch it. It would serve him right if she used his money to buy something in outrageously bad taste, but of course she couldn't do that to herself. And as for asking Alesi to help her choose her outfit, she seethed, that was the last thing she would do! If she asked anyone's opinion it would be Maria's.

The week ahead seemed to stretch interminably before her as Liv wished it past, but surprisingly the days flew by. The shop was exceptionally busy considering it was off season, and on Thursday Melly fell down at school and had to have three stitches inserted in a gash in her arm. In between all this Liv managed to finish two canvases which she had been commissioned to do before Ryan's return.

Joel called to see her on Wednesday agog with the news of Ryan's purchase of Craven Island. Both Joel and D.J. had received an invitation to the dinner.

'I still can't believe he's bought the island,' Joel shook his head. 'I mean, he always used to talk about it in the old days, but D.J. would never listen to his ideas. It used to drive Ryan crazy and eventually he stopped mentioning it. I thought he'd forgotten about it.'

'How did D.J. take the news?' Liv asked.

'Calmly, so far.' Joel crossed his fingers. 'He was sort of stunned at first and now he's being very cool and not saying a thing. What worries me is that I suspect he has an idea that Ryan bought the island to add to the family enterprises,' Joel grimaced, 'and if I know Ryan nothing could be further from the truth. Ryan's no fool and he knows D.J. If he lets him near the project it will be another D. J. Denison scheme. Or perhaps—and mind, I say perhaps—D.J.'s mellowing at last. Did Ryan outline any of his plans to you?'

'No, not really. But he wants me to be a hostess at the dinner and I wish I knew why. Knowing Ryan, there has to be something behind it.'

'I guess all we can do is sit back and wait for it all to unfold,' said Joel, smiling. 'It should be interesting to see how everyone reacts.'

Before she knew it Liv was heading homewards after collecting the twins from the Costellos'. The children were looking forward to their evening on the yacht and chattered excitedly as they showered and changed to be ready by six-thirty.

If Liv's mind had turned to their proposed discussion with the twins then she had shied away from even thinking about it. Now she was almost trembling with nervousness and a hopeless kind of dread. She was still no closer to knowing the best way of broaching the subject. Although Luke hadn't asked any more questions and his attitude towards Ryan seemed to have undergone a subtle tempering, she was worried about his reaction to the knowledge that Ryan was his father. As far as her daughter was concerned Liv could see no problems. Melly had fallen for Ryan's charm almost from the first.

'He's here, Mummy,' called Melly, racing from her vantage point at the living room window to the front door and smiling at Ryan as he walked up the steps. 'Mummy's nearly ready,' she told him.

Nervously Liv gave her hair a final brush before securing it neatly at the nape of her neck. She wore a dark green scrub denim suit of flared slacks and a long-sleeved shirt jacket. Ryan's gaze moved over her as she joined them and his eyes settled for a moment on her sedate hair-style before he turned to follow the twins out to the car. It was on the tip of Liv's tongue to tell him she had tied it back because of the wind and not because he had stated his preference for her to leave it hanging loosely about her shoulders. But she restrained herself and walked silently after him.

He was wearing a pair of grey tailored slacks and a soft white terry towelling windcheater, the rope ties at the neck hanging casually open, and Liv turned away from his compelling handsomeness. And there was no denying his attractiveness. It rose within her to catch her and her heart pulsed with a dull ache. But tonight she must keep a cool head, remain calm and composed, be reassuring so that the twins didn't sense her uncertainty or antipathy.

'Relax,' said Ryan quietly as he held the door open for her. 'They're intelligent kids, they'll understand.'

'I wish I felt as confident,' she replied shakily.

Instead of being moored at the wharf the yacht was anchored out in the bay and they made their way out to it in a small outboard motor-driven dinghy. The breeze was stiff with the sea just a little choppy and Liv looked uneasily at the clouds in the sky.

'We could have a shower before morning,' Ryan raised his voice above the noise of the outboard motor, 'but according to the weather report it should be fine tomorrow.'

Liv's thoughts returned to the last time she had been aboard the *Midnight Blue* during a tropical shower and she shivered involuntarily. At least tonight they were only staying on board for a couple of hours.

'Where are Alesi and Roko?' asked Luke as he watched Ryan make fast the dinghy. 'I thought Roko might play his guitar for us again tonight.'

'They've gone ashore visiting for a couple of days,' said Ryan, 'so there's just us.'

'Are you making our dinner again?' asked Melly, gazing up at Ryan with a look almost bordering on adoration.

Liv felt the pain twist inside her. She had been younger than Melly when she had first looked up at him with just such a look on her face.

'Sure am. Hope everyone likes Chinese food,' he said, and opened the cabin hatch for them to go below.

The meal was delicious. Ryan had most of it prepared and they sat chatting to him while he put his concoction together. At least the twins and Ryan kept up a lively conversation about school, Luke's soccer and Melly's dancing lessoons and, of course, Melly held up her patched arm for inspection, giving Ryan a very detailed and gory account of the accident. Liv sat silently listening and worrying, seeing all kinds of traumatic situations resulting from the next few hours.

Ryan accepted the children's compliments on his culinary skill and his eyes moved questioningly to Liv. 'How about it, Liv? Enjoy your dinner?'

'Yes, thank you. It was very nice,' she replied truthfully. 'Where did you learn to cook?'

'Oh, I picked up a bit here and a little there,' he grinned.

'When you were sailing about the world?' Melly's eyes were large.

'Something like that,' he laughed.

'I'll bet you had lots of adventures,' said Luke. 'Did you ever get shipwrecked like Robinson Crusoe?'

'No, I'm afraid not,' Ryan replied sadly.

'Not even once?' sighed Luke disappointedly. 'What was your biggest adventure, then?' he pursued his point.

'Well, it wasn't exactly an adventure, but the worst moment I ever experienced was landing a small plane on a beach when the engine began to play up. I made it down all right, but I ran out of hard sand when I had to swerve around some rocks. The wheels bogged down and she tipped up on her nose. The hardest part was climbing out of my seat at that angle.'

'What happened to the plane? Did you leave it on the beach?' asked Luke.

'No. We fixed it up and flew it out.'

'Do you fly planes, too?' Melly asked. 'Gee, you must be able to do everything!'

'I wouldn't say I could do everything, Melly,' his eyes turned to Liv mockingly. 'There are lots of things I couldn't do. Like painting as well as your mother does.'

The twins looked at Liv.

'Yes, Mum is good at painting. She even painted pictures of us and gave them to Grandfather,' Luke said proudly. 'Would you like her to paint one of you?'

'That would be a challenge, Liv?' he said drily, lifting one dark eyebrow.

'Portraits aren't exactly my forte,' Liv replied. 'I much prefer land and seascapes.'

'Luke can draw very well, too, just like Mummy can,' said Melly, adding dejectedly, 'but I can't.'

'You're better at spelling than I am,' said Luke generously, and Ryan's lips twitched. 'Grandfather says there are some things that some people can do and some things that other people can do, so if everybody does what they can do then everything will get done eventually,' said Luke, and a thoughtful frown touched his face. 'Grandfather Denison is your father, isn't he?' His question took both Liv and Ryan by surprise.

'Yes, he is,' replied Ryan easily.

'Why did you go away? Couldn't you get a job, like Danny's father? Danny used to play with Dino and me, but had to go to Gladstone 'cause his father couldn't find a job here.'

'I did have a job, but I wanted to have a try at working for myself. The kind of work I wanted to do I couldn't do around here. Do you understand what I mean?' Ryan explained.

Luke nodded. 'Are you married?' he asked quickly, as though he had psyched himself up to ask the question.

Liv's face was hot and she felt Ryan's eyes on her before he answered.

'Yes, I'm married.'

Luke picked up his fork and put it down again, his young face serious. 'Are you really our father?' he asked quietly.

'Luke, you said we weren't to say anything about that,' Melly's lip trembled. 'You said Mummy might get upset.' She turned swimming eyes on Liv to see if this was so.

Now that he had put to Ryan the question that had obviously been discussed by both of them some of the bravado had gone from Luke's face, leaving him looking young and vulnerable, a child putting a tentative foot into an adult world.

'Would *you* be upset if I told you that your mother and I were married and that I was your father?' Ryan asked them quietly.

'I think you'd be a very nice father,' said Melly, sniffing.

Ryan smiled at her and turned his gaze on his son. 'How about you, Luke?'

'I guess it would be okay with us if it's okay with Mum.' He glanced sideways at Liv, whose throat was choked on a sob she refused to allow to escape. 'But why did you leave us?' he asked, looking levelly at Ryan.

'Luke . . .' Liv began, but Ryan silenced her with a shake of his head.

'That's a fair question, Luke. I had what I thought were very good reasons for going at the time, but it may be just a little hard for me to explain to you just now,' he began. 'Adults make mistakes, too, and they often do and say things that children find it hard to understand.'

'Did you have a fight?' asked Melly.

'Something like that.'

'Will you be staying here now?' Luke asked.

Ryan paused. 'I don't know, Luke. But while I'm here I'd like us all to be friends, get to know one another. What do you say?'

'Mum?' Luke turned to his mother. 'Is it okay with you?'

'Of course.'

'Now we won't be the only kids in class without a daddy,' smiled Melly, and Liv turned pain-filled eyes on her daughter. She hadn't even known that the twins had so much as thought about that aspect.

Luke smiled crookedly at her, his face flushed. 'It wasn't so bad really, Mum. Some of the kids' fathers were pretty tough on them,' he grinned. 'And besides, we always had Uncle Joel.'

'Joel has been very good to us,' Liv told Ryan. 'He's a wonderful person.'

Ryan made no comment on that and began to collect their dinner plates together. 'Who's for dessert? I don't suppose anyone likes icecream?'

The evening passed quickly and pleasantly and any strained moments that rose between the adults went unnoticed by the children. When she realised they were beginning to yawn Liv suggested that perhaps they should be going. She felt emotionally drained herself now that it was all over. As if on cue the rain fell.

Ryan opened the cabin door and quickly closed it again. 'You'd get soaked to the skin in seconds if we left now. I'll have to ship and cover the dinghy so it doesn't wallow and sink.' He hurried into the stern cabin and returned wearing his brief swim shorts.

'Do you need any help?' Liv asked him.

'No, I can manage, thanks. I'll only be a few minutes.'

When he returned it appeared to be raining even harder and Liv handed him a towel to dry himself off.

'Doesn't look like easing up for some time,' he said, rubbing his hair. 'Why don't you stay on board tonight?'

Liv's chin lifted and her eyes met his. She wouldn't put it past him to have conjured up this bad weather, she thought wryly.

'You and Melly can take the stern cabin and Luke and I can share the forward one,' he added mockingly.

'Hey! Great!' grinned Luke.

'But we haven't brought our pyjamas,' said Melly, horrified.

Ryan raised his eyebrows. 'You can sleep in your undies and T-shirt and I'll lend your mother one of my shirts.'

'A shirt?' Melly giggled, putting one dimpled hand over her mouth. 'You'll look funny, Mummy.'

'We . . . we'll have to leave fairly early in the morning,' put in Liv, 'as Luke has to play soccer.'

'Maybe you could—well, come along and watch the game if you'd like to, if you're not going to be busy.' Luke's cheeks were tinged with red as he glanced at his father. 'Some of the guys play really well.'

'I think Luke plays the best,' put in Melly, and her brother's face grew even redder.

'Sometimes Uncle Joel and Grandfather come, too,' he added.

'I'd like that very much,' he said, and had turned away before Liv could see if he really meant what he said.

'Dino plays on my team, too,' Luke informed him. 'And so do a couple of other kids from my class at school. And Aunt Maria and Uncle Mike usually go to watch the game as well.'

'Sounds like you enjoy playing,' Ryan ruffled Luke's hair.

'It's really great,' beamed Luke.

'I'll collect my clothes from the cabin and I'll shower up front.' Ryan rubbed the mat of dark hair on his chest with the towel. 'I won't be a moment.'

'Come on, Luke, I'll tuck you up before Melly and I settle down.' Liv took the opposite cabinway to Ryan.

'Was it all right to ask . . .?' Luke paused and lowered his voice. 'Do you think he'll mind if we call him Dad?'

'No. No, I'm sure he won't mind if that's what you want.' Liv busied herself tucking the blanket under the mattress.

'Oh, good. Was it all right to ask Dad along to watch me play soccer?' he asked, watching his mother's face.

'Of course. But you must remember your . . . your father's a busy man and he may not always be free to come along every time you ask him.' She leant over and kissed him. 'Luke, how did you find out about your father? Did someone tell you?'

'Well, not exactly.' He looked a little sheepish. 'Dino heard someone talking about it at school and he asked me and we kind of worked it out.'

'Oh, I see.'

'You're not angry, are you, Mum?'

'No, of course not,' she smiled at him. 'Well, off to sleep, love. See you in the morning.'

Liv walked slowly back to the stern cabin and she

could hear Melly's giggle as she stepped down into the hallway.

'Daddy's picked out a shirt for you,' she said, 'and it's got a Fijian house on it. Isn't it pretty?' She held it up.

'Thank you.' Liv left her eyes on his chin, not wanting to read the expression she knew would be in his eyes, and that same tension filled the room.

'No sweat. I'll see you in the morning.' He went to step past Liv and she could see the tightness in his jaw.

'Daddy?'

Ryan stopped in mid-stride and for a moment Liv thought she saw a flash of pain in his eyes before he turned back to Melly.

'Aren't you going to kiss me goodnight?' Melly sprang on to the bed and dived between the sheets. 'Mummy always kisses us goodnight.'

Ryan bent over the bed and Melly's arms wrapped around his neck, giving him a hug. 'It's nice having a daddy.'

'And it's nice being a daddy,' he said simply, and turned to Liv, his expression guarded. 'How about Mummy? Does she want a kiss goodnight, too?'

'No, thank you,' Liv said stiffly. The very last thing she wanted was to feel the touch of his near-naked body against her.

'But I insist,' he said, and his cool lips descended on hers in a too brief, far too circumspect kiss, which only served to whet her appetite for a more intimate caress. 'Goodnight, Liv,' he said, and quietly left them.

Dressed in Ryan's T-shirt, bringing the subtle odour of his body to tease her senses, Liv lay awake on the same bunk she had had on their trip to Craven Island, wishing that he lay beside her as he had done on that night. She wanted to feel the warmth of his undoubted strength.

In the seven years since the birth of the twins she had never once shirked her responsibilities towards them. And the responsibilities of caring for two small children had not been an easy task for a seventeen-year-old girl who had been so totally disillusioned with life.

Tonight Liv had felt the weight of those responsibilities, a weight she had been unaware she carried, lighten considerably. It was a comforting feeling to know that there was someone else there, that he could be there if she needed him.

Although she had depended a lot on Joel, especially after her father died, she had still basically borne the worries and anxieties by herself, and the urge to give in, to just allow herself to lean on Ryan, swept over her in a surge of longing.

Perhaps she did need him, need someone, to help in the making of decisions where the children were concerned, even more so as they grew older. All she had to do was to go to him now, tell him she wanted . . .

But was that what Ryan wanted? He had said at first that he wanted them with him, but did he realise exactly what he would be taking on? Would the strain of having an instant family have him leaving again? Last week he had said he might leave once the resort got under way. Liv had to think of the effect such a parting might have on the children and on herself. To have Ryan's strength for a short time and then to lose it would be all but unbearable. The break this time would be even more crushing than it had been eight years ago. No, she just couldn't afford to take the chance. She would have to steel herself against him, discipline her traitorous body and remind herself constantly that he was still the same spoilt, irresponsible boy, now an even more dangerous and potent man.

Liv woke early, the darkness only tinged with light, and, gazing out through her porthole at the dusky sky, she could see that the rain had gone. Stretching tiredly, for she had tossed restlessly for part of the night, she climbed out of bed and quietly moved on bare feet into the bathroom. Her face washed in cold water banished some of her fuzzy-headedness and she padded into the galley for a drink of milk.

She was rinsing and drying the glass she had used when a soft sound behind her had her spinning around. Ryan stood leaning in the cabinway, wearing only brief denim shorts, his hair tousled and the dark shadow of a beard on his unshaven jaw.

'I thought I heard a noise out here and I came out in case it was Melly.'

'No. She's still sound asleep.' Liv's heart was in her mouth as she gazed at the tanned firmness of his body.

'So is Luke,' he said, rubbing a hand over his roughened cheek.

'I was just having a glass of milk.'

He nodded, his eyes moving over her body clad in his slightly misshapen T-shirt, lingering on the long length of her legs. 'That shirt definitely looks better on you than it does on me.' His tone was a caress.

Liv could feel the volatile tension rising between them and knew she had to escape from the explosiveness of the atmosphere. 'I'll get back to bed for another hour or so.'

'Did you sleep well?' He had moved closer.

'Yes, thank you. Ryan . . .'

'Aren't you going to ask me how I slept?'

Liv's gaze was drawn to his red-rimmed eyes.

'Well, I didn't—sleep, that is. Something kept disturbing me,' he smiled self-derisively. 'I kept thinking about you, seeing you in that damn shirt, and sleep was the last thing on my mind.'

'Ryan, last night you said . . .' Liv backed away from him, but he followed, although he didn't touch her.

'I know what I said last night. I must have been mad.' He ran a hand through his hair. 'God, do you know what it was like lying up there, knowing you were so near, wanting you like crazy?' His voice was thick and low and his hand moved to cup her cheek. 'I don't suppose you'd care to change your mind about the sleeping arrangements?' he said huskily.

Liv's heart fluttered. Dear God, if he only knew how much she wanted to say yes! But if she gave in to him she would be like putty in his hands. He could mould her, and when the time came for him to leave he would go without a backward glance, as he had done before. She hardened her resolution. 'No, Ryan,' she said firmly.

He drew a deep breath and she could see the conflict in his eyes, in the throb of the pulse in his hair-roughened jaw, before he turned sharply away.

'You'd better get back to bed, then,' he said tightly, 'before I change my mind and decide to help you change yours.'

CHAPTER NINE

RYAN had to go down to Brisbane again, so they didn't see him in the next week, and for that Liv was profoundly grateful. The more she saw of him the more vulnerable she became, and she was in no hurry to put to the test her new resolution to keep herself aloof from him for fear that her resolve broke down and failed her.

However, with Maria's help, she did buy herself a new dress for the dinner. Taking Ryan at his word, she had chosen a very slinky, very exclusive and very expensive creation.

She had tried on a half dozen or more dresses before Maria spied a black one hanging at the far end of the rack and she held it up for Liv almost with reverence.

'This is it, Liv. It's just the dress for you. I can't wait for you to try it on!' And she had Liv zipped into the dress before she could turn around.

And Maria was right. The dress was made for her and didn't need as much as an alteration to the hemline. The neck plunged only low enough in the front to display the beginnings of the rounded swell of her breasts but not deeply enough to be considered in bad taste. Meanwhile the back was scooped to expose her smooth tanned skin.

The fitted bodice moulded her breasts and from the narrowness of her waist it fell to the floor in folds of shimmering black gossamer. It was a perfect foil for her blue eyes and silky fair hair, but the price tag made her gasp.

Maria waved her protests aside, reminding her that Ryan was paying for the dress and that by all accounts he could afford it, and they left the boutique with the sleekly wrapped box under Liv's arm.

And now, as she dressed for the evening, having taken the twins over to Maria's earlier, she was glad of the elegance of the dress, knowing she would be able to gain some confidence from the fact that it suited her and that a little of her nervousness and misgivings would be quelled by that knowledge.

She also felt easier because Ryan would not be calling for her. He had telephoned to make his apologies. He would be tied up for a couple of hours with some unforeseen last-minute preparations for the evening, so it was Joel who would be collecting her at seven-thirty to escort her to the hotel at Airlie Beach.

Her make-up had been applied, a little blue eye-shadow and mascara and some pale pink lipstick, and her hair shone like spun gold. She had decided to let it fall loosely about her face and shoulders in its natural waves after considering piling it up on top of her head in a mass of curls. But she knew she would feel uncomfortable trying to carry off such statuesque sophistication. The only way she could cope with the evening was to try to relax and be herself. To attempt to uphold any other pose would make the evening even more nerve-racking.

Picking up her wristwatch from the dressing table, she saw it was almost time for Joel to arrive and a tiny fluttering of butterflies stirred inside her. She half wished now that she had refused Ryan's invitation, but she had accepted, so now she must see the evening through.

'You know, you're really going to stun everyone tonight, Liv,' Joel remarked, taking her arm as they walked into the lobby of the hotel. 'I've never seen you looking so attractive. Not that you aren't always attractive,' he laughed, 'but tonight—wow!' He touched his fingers to his lips. 'That dress is fantastic, really fantastic!'

'And I'll bet you've been practising that little speech all the way here,' Liv chided him, not un-affected by his obviously genuine compliments. 'The wrapping may be a little more chic, more expensive, a lot more expensive,' she added emphatically, 'but the package inside is still the same old me. I just hope this is the type of outfit Ryan had in mind when he asked me to act as a hostess.'

'Oh, that outfit is what every man has on his mind at some time or other, believe me,' chuckled Joel. 'You'll do wonders for my ego. Every guy will be green with envy when I escort you into the convention room,' he straightened his bow tie, 'including brother Ryan, which won't hurt him for once. What do you say?'

'I say you're ever the romantic, Joel Denison,' said Liv drily, 'with just a dash of the tooth fairy.'

Joel laughed again, stopping before the doorway to smooth the lapels of his jacket. 'Well, here we go. If Ryan's depending on you to sell his ideas to the locals, then it's a foregone conclusion.' He winked at her and patted the hand resting on his arm and they entered the convention centre.

The room was quite large and seemed to be swarm-ing with guests already. Liv recognised most of those present. There was the mayor and a number of councillors and their wives, the owners and managers of various local businesses and a sprinkling of professional people.

They eyed Liv's appearance with Joel with avid interest, and the couple had only taken a few steps into the room before they were stopped by friendly greetings. Of course Joel was popular with everyone in the district, but Liv wondered rather cynically how much of the attention they were being afforded was due to an eagerness to find out whether there had been a reconciliation between Ryan and herself. Not that anyone asked any impertinent questions, quite the contrary. No comment was made, but glances moved curiously from Liv and Joel to Ryan.

It wasn't long before Ryan excused himself from a group of people and strode purposefully across towards them. Of course, she had placed him immediately she had entered the room. She seemed to have some form of sonar system where he was concerned. He wore a dark immaculately cut suit and a pale shirt with a conservative tie and looked as handsome, as debonair, as he always did. But tonight he also exuded an air of trustworthiness, of dependability. Yes, he looked as successful as he obviously was, and Liv could sense that most of the guests were impressed.

As everyone watched surreptitiously he shook hands with Joel and drew Liv's hand into the crook of his arm, bringing her close to his side. 'Joel, thanks for collecting Liv. Come and meet a friend and associate of mine.'

Joel's quick wink at Liv as they strolled along with

Ryan did nothing for the state of Liv's churning stomach. Ryan's hold blatantly said possession and when Liv went to remove her arm he clasped it firmly to his side, his expression not even flickering.

They rejoined the group of people to whom Ryan had been talking when Joel and Liv arrived and Liv noticed for the first time that D.J. was also part of the group. Roko was there, looking incongruous in a suit, and there was also another Fijian standing between him and D.J.

Ryan's smile was pleasant. 'Kim, meet my brother Joel, and,' he pulled Liv even closer, smiling down at her, setting her senses spinning again, 'Liv, my wife. Darling, this is Kim Sukuna, an associate of mine and a great friend.'

As the men shook hands Liv noticed that Roko was staring at Ryan as though he had gone mad. 'You and Liv are married?'

'Yes. We've spent some time apart, but now we'll be able to see so much more of each other,' Ryan replied easily.

'May I call you Liv?' asked the older man, 'and you must call me Kim.' His teeth flashed white and humorously in his dark face. 'I would have recognised you anywhere, Liv, from the photograph Ryan carries with him. I feel I know you already.'

Liv's eyebrows rose enquiringly.

'Ryan spoke to me of you often over the years,' he said.

Joel caught Liv's eye and he had 'I told you so' written all over his face.

'I believe you have two beautiful children as well,' Kim was saying.

'Yes. Yes, I . . . we do. A boy and a girl,' she said breathlessly.

'Ah, a pigeon pair.' Kim smiled. 'Like my wife and me. We have a daughter a little younger than my son Roko here.' Kim put a hand on Roko's shoulder.

It was Liv's turn to be shocked. 'You scarcely look old enough to be Roko's father, Mr Suk . . . Kim.'

He laughed gaily and Roko joined in. 'Thank you, Liv. My wife complains that she has been given the wrinkles for both of us but, believe me, she doesn't look very much older than our daughter or my niece, Alesi.'

At the mention of Alesi's name Liv cast a quick look around for the other girl and saw her talking to a group of younger people. The Fijian girl looked exceptionally beautiful, her dark skin a perfect contrast to her white hostess dress which had been screen printed with colourful designs of hibiscus flowers. Had Ryan told her that he was married to Liv or was he leaving her to find out in the same manner as Roko? Surely if there was any relationship between them Ryan would find a less painful way of informing Alesi.

'Is your wife with you?' Joel was asking Kim.

'Alas, no. She has had to remain in Suva for a week or two. Our daughter has recently given birth to our first grandchild and my wife felt she must be by her side for a little time.' He turned to D.J. 'It's a good feeling to have a grandchild to follow you in life, don't you think, Mr Denison?'

'Yes.' D.J. looked into the glass of Scotch he was drinking. 'Yes. I'm very proud of my two grandchildren,' he said smiling faintly at Liv.

Was everyone going mad? she asked herself. Never had she seen D.J. so subdued, so complacent.

The meal provided was delicious by any standards, with the number of guests being about two hundred, Liv estimated, and the whole evening appeared to be going off without a hitch. Liv found herself seated between the mayor and another senior councilman who turned out to be an acquaintance of her father's.

It was only after the meal that the business of the evening was mentioned and Ryan and Kim Sukuna outlined the plans they had for the development of Craven Island into a tourist resort. The scheme was to be financed by Ryan and he would have two assistants on the management side of the business. Kim Sukuna was to be in charge of the accommodation and dining sections while a Canadian, Scott Mallory, would supervise the special section devoted especially to children. Ryan apologised for the absence of the Canadian whose aircraft had been held up en route from Vancouver.

Listening intently to Ryan outlining his objectives, Liv had to admit that she was impressed, as impressed as everyone else appeared to be. The resort was to focus on the family, with as much emphasis being placed on providing a holiday that children could enjoy as much as their parents. And the parents could choose to spend their time with their children or without them, knowing in the latter case that their children were under qualified supervision.

While their parents were accommodated in the main complex the children would have the opportunity to camp out, to be instructed in the arts of bushcraft, camp cooking, could go hiking or simply share the other facilities with their parents.

Scott Mallory came well recommended from various positions in summer camps in the United States and Canada and Alesi Sukuna, who Liv learned was a trained nurse, was to be his assistant.

Many positions would be available for the local people to work on the island and all in all the complex could only benefit the community and the area. And the majority of the guests were in favour of the project. Liv could sense their interest and excitement.

However, when Ryan invited questions, a small faction began to put forward reasons against the project and Liv was astounded when she recognised one of the protesters as Martin Wilson. She hadn't seen him or heard from him since the evening Ryan had so blatantly introduced himself and she wasn't even aware that he had been attending the function.

Ryan answered their negative views honestly and knowledgeably and after a time they gave up their attempts to thwart the project. Ryan had done his homework far too well for a few half-hearted protesters to discompose him.

The mayor seemed well pleased with the affair and said as much to Liv. 'You know, Mrs Denison, we need family-orientated amusements and it seems your husband agrees with me on this. Being a family man himself he can stand as a solid recommendation for the project.'

As she watched Ryan as he stood discussing some point raised by one of the councillors a thought struck Liv like a blow. Could that have been the real reason he wanted them back? So that he could show himself as a good example for his family resort? An icy hand clutched her heart. Surely even he couldn't cold-bloodedly go to those lengths to get what he wanted?

Later everyone moved among the maps, plans and models of the proposed development that were on display while Ryan mingled confidently pointing out certain sections to illustrate his proposals.

'Well, Liv, your husband seems to be doing all right for himself tonight.' Martin materialised out of the crowd, looking just a little flushed.

'Yes. He's certainly put a lot of thought and effort into the project,' she said, looking about for an excuse to move on.

'As they say, money speaks all languages,' Martin ran a finger around the inside of his collar, 'and it's a very juicy bait when you're trying to hook the fish.'

'What are you talking about, Martin?' Liv began to suspect he had had too much to drink.

'Well, he's making promises of more money for the business community, more jobs for the local work force and last, but not least, luxury for you.'

'Luxury for . . . Just what are you trying to say to me, Martin?'

'That perhaps a lowly schoolteacher isn't good enough any more. Maybe you have bigger fish to fry?'

'You're being ridiculous, Martin. I never made any promises to you, and you know it,' Liv bit out angrily.

'What seems to be the trouble, Liv?' Joel asked evenly as he joined them, noting Liv's set expression and Martin's flushed face.

'Ah, Joel,' Liv felt like hugging him. 'Martin was just about to move on.' She turned from him. 'Is that a spare glass of champagne?' she asked, taking the glass Joel held out to her.

'What was all that about?' asked Joel as Martin walked stiffly away.

'Oh, nothing much.' Liv took a sip of the bubbly liquid. 'He was being spiteful and—well . . .'

'And you're well rid of him,' grinned Joel as he turned to survey the room. 'Looks like another successful development.'

'I get that feeling, too. Did you doubt it?' she asked drily, taking another steadying sip of her champagne and wrinkling her nose as the bubbles rose to tickle it.

'Not really. I think the ideas are great and, as I said, Ryan used to talk of nothing else years ago. D.J.'s taking it all very well, isn't he? He's most subdued. Do you suppose he's mellowing at last?' Joel grinned. 'Or perhaps Ryan's finally made it into the grown-up world.'

'And what about you, Joel?' Liv smiled.

'Me? I'm still a boy,' he grimaced. 'Don't worry, Liv. I'm quite happy. He's not as rough on me as he was on Ryan. I guess their like personalities repel.'

'Joel, introduce me to this divine creature.'

Neither Joel nor Liv had noticed the young man approaching them until he spoke and Liv flushed under his openly admiring face.

'Hey, Scott! When did you arrive?' Joel shook the other man's hand.

He was as tall as Joel with dark curly hair not quite long enough to be called Afro and he sported a fashionably shaped moustache.

'I made it here about fifteen minutes ago. My plane was late and I missed my connection in

Sydney.' He spoke with a slightly moderated American accent. 'I would have been livid had I known just what I was missing up here,' he turned sparkling brown eyes, the lids slightly red from jet lag, back to Liv.

'You obviously haven't changed much over the years, Scotty. Still masquerading as a playboy?' Joel laughed.

'Enough of that! You'll spoil my image with the most beautiful girl I've ever set eyes on in my life.'

Joel glanced skywards and picked up Liv's left hand, displaying her gold wedding band. 'Sorry to have to be the one to break it to you, mate. Meet my sister-in-law, Liv Denison. This Don Juan is Scott Mallory. Ryan and I met him in Quebec when we were on holiday there ten or eleven years ago.'

Scott gave Liv's ring a rueful glance and shrugged his shoulders. 'Oh well, all's fair in love and war. I'll take advantage of your husband's absence to express my deepest regrets that I didn't meet you before he did.'

Liv laughed easily, not taking offence at his good-natured flirting.

'How did you come to go into this resort with Ryan?' asked Joel.

'I met up with him again in the States two years ago and he sounded me out about giving the idea a try.' He drew his eyes from Liv. 'I liked his proposals and I wanted to see Australia. Besides, Ryan always did mean to go places and he will. This will be a huge success.'

'Sure to be,' agreed Joel as Scott turned back to Liv.

'Tell me, what position will your husband hold, Liv? I guess he's in on this, too.' He frowned. 'You know, I could have sworn Ryan only had one brother.'

'Well, Scott, I see you made it,' Ryan joined them. 'Did I hear my name mentioned?' he asked, shaking hands with the Canadian.

'Yes, you surely did. I was asking Liv which Denison had managed to capture her.'

Joel laughed. 'Shall we put him out of his misery?' His glance took in both Liv and his brother.

Ryan's facial expression barely altered, but his eyes became guarded, watchful. 'Sorry, Scott. Hands off,' he said pleasantly enough. 'Liv happens to be married to me.'

'You? I didn't even know you were married.' Scott Mallory couldn't hide his surprise. 'You have to be newlyweds, then.'

'Eight years, actually,' answered Ryan, his arm moving around Liv's waist in that same gesture of possession.

Liv felt her hackles rise. Here she was standing about like a piece of merchandise, ready to be haggled over.

'As a matter of fact, she married brother Ryan because she couldn't have me,' Joel chuckled. 'Didn't you, Liv?'

She laughed with him, if somewhat wryly. 'My first big mistake, Joel,' she said, and felt Ryan's fingers tighten on her waist.

'I'm afraid I must spirit her away for a moment,' said Ryan. 'See you both later. Joel can introduce you round, Scott.'

With his hand firmly on her arm Liv was soon whisked away into a small alcove off the main room.

'How do you think things are going?' Ryan stood with his hands in his pockets.

'Very well,' Liv replied. 'But then you don't need me to tell you that,' she added, knowing that wasn't what he had brought her here to ask her. His face had that closed look and she could feel he was choosing his words, words she suspected she wouldn't want to hear.

A sudden wave of depression crept over her. He looked so large and attractive standing there and she wished again that things had been different between them, that there had been a mutual bond of love to hold them together instead of this guarded, furtive watching of each other in which they seemed to indulge.

'I gather you're very taken with Scott Mallory?' he said at last.

'He seems very nice,' said Liv, surprised.

'Nice?' His tone changed the meaning of the word considerably.

'Yes. Nice. And very friendly.' Liv's mouth set. 'I've only met him in the last ten minutes or so and I've scarcely exchanged more than a few words with the man, so on that basis I'd say nice and friendly.'

'I'd prefer it if you were to keep him at arm's length, if you don't mind,' Ryan said softly.

'And if I do mind?' Liv raised her chin.

'I don't need any complications of that nature before we even get under way.'

'Complications of what nature in particular?' Liv asked with deceptive calmness.

'You know what I mean. I've known Scott a long time. He's something of a ladies' man, has a girl in every town. I wouldn't want you to get the wrong idea about his attentions,' he said, his eyes narrowed.

'The wrong idea?' she repeated incredulously. 'For heaven's sake, Ryan, credit me with a little common sense! I've managed over the years to get by on my own judgement of a person's character. I can recognise a wolf when I see one and I'd say your friend is one of the likeable and harmless ones.'

Ryan gave a short laugh.

'I assure you, I've come a long way in eight years and I'm not about to fall into his or anyone else's arms.' Her anger rose and she knew a desire to slap his handsome face and was goaded into adding, 'Or is that the whole trouble, Ryan? Sour grapes because I haven't fallen easily into your arms?'

'Liv, you're pushing me and I won't . . .'

'There you are, Ryan.' Roko Sukuna stuck his head into the alcove and Ryan's hand fell from Liv's arm as he turned from her. 'The old lady, Mrs Craven, she wants to see you and Liv now before she leaves.'

'All right, Roko, we're coming.' He stood back for Liv to precede him into the convention room, although he didn't take her arm as they followed Roko across the floor.

Mrs Craven smiled tiredly as they approached and Liv hastily subdued her anger.

'Well, Ryan, you've got everybody on your side at last,' she shook her white head, 'just as you said you would all those years ago.' Her bright alert eyes turned to the girl at Ryan's side. 'You have a very determined husband here, Liv. It must be all of ten years ago that he told me the plans he had for a family resort on Craven Island if I could see my way to sell it to him. And I told him if he came to me with the money and could prove to me that he'd settled down at last then the island was his.' She turned back to Ryan. 'You've realised the first stage of your dream. I'm looking forward to seeing the finished product.'

'Not half as much as I am.' Ryan smiled down at the old woman with that same smile he used with the twins and Liv's heart lurched painfully. He used to smile at her like that once. But no more.

'Well, I must be getting my tired bones home to bed. This is a late night for me and I'm not used to late nights now. I'm happy to see you and Ryan back together again, Liv. You must bring the children to see me one day. As a matter of fact, when Ryan told me you'd patched up your differences—well, it put the seal on our transaction. I'm a firm believer in a good marriage making a good man. Ryan reminds me of my late husband and although he's not here to deny it he needed me to keep him on an even keel,' she laughed, and Ryan smiled as he took her arm to help her up.

'I'll walk you out to your taxi,' he said. 'You'll excuse me, Liv?' His eyes didn't reach hers as she stood speechless.

'Goodnight, my dear,' Mrs Craven patted Liv's arm, unaware of the turmoil in Liv's mind. 'He's a handsome devil, isn't he?' She inclined her head in Ryan's direction. 'If I was forty years younger I'd be giving you a run for your money where this young man is concerned,' she winked at Ryan. 'Remember to come to see me, child, if you have a spare hour or two.'

Liv stood watching Ryan supporting the old lady's

steps through the crowd, his dark hair shining in the artificial lights as he bent to listen to something Mrs Craven was saying. In that moment her whole body felt numb.

So that was the reason Ryan had wanted her here tonight. To prove to the old lady that what he'd told her was the truth, that they had been reconciled. He had manipulated her and the children to cement the sale of the property which countless numbers of developers and speculators had coveted for years. Ryan had taken advantage of her again. She might have guessed as much.

The pain these revelations brought with them touched a raw nerve within her and spread throughout her body until she turned to the table against the wall and breathlessly poured herself a chilled fruit juice in an effort to disguise her agitation. Standing making a pretence of sipping the drink, she prayed that no one would notice her pallor. She couldn't bear an inquisition at this moment.

Although she chided herself angrily for her gullibility it didn't seem to help. The pain was deep and devastating and refused to subside. Inwardly she cursed herself for being all kinds of a fool. Ryan had always been ruthless; why should she have thought he could have changed? Hadn't he always used everyone to get what he wanted? Well, he'd done it again.

She couldn't remain here a minute longer, and to set eyes on Ryan again tonight would only intensify her anger, her hurt. Joel would take her home. Decided, she replaced her barely touched glass of juice on the table and turned to scan the crowded room for her brother-in-law. He was nowhere to be seen. By the time she had walked from one end of the room to the other she was certain he wasn't there. And neither was Scott Mallory or her father-in-law, for that matter. Maybe she'd missed them.

'Lost someone, Olivia?' Martin asked, looking more like his normal self. His anger had cooled and his heightened colour had subsided.

'I can't seem to find Joel. I don't suppose you've seen him, have you?' she asked, frowning.

'He left a couple of minutes ago, apparently to drive your father-in-law home. They had someone else with them, a tall dark bushy-haired fellow.'

'That would be Scott Mallory. Oh, dear, I was going to ask Joel to drive me home. I . . . I seem to have developed a slight headache,' she said, realising she was speaking the truth. She could feel an aching behind her eyes.

'I'll drive you home if you'd like,' Martin offered.

Liv regarded him carefully. Earlier in the evening she had suspected he had been drinking, but he seemed quite sober now. Maybe his anger had been responsible for his slight incoherence. However, she'd better wait for Joel to return.

'Thanks all the same, Martin, I can last out until Joel comes back,' she smiled.

'It's no trouble, Olivia, I was leaving myself anyway.'

'Well—' Liv hesitated before capitulating. 'All right. I'll just tell Kim Sukuna I'm leaving so Joel will know I've had a lift home.'

'Fine. I'll wait for you at the door.'

In the crowd it took Liv several minutes to locate Kim and as she moved back towards Martin a sense of inevitability swept over her as Ryan appeared in the doorway, his eyes moving quickly from Martin to her.

'Ready, Olivia?' Martin asked.

'Yes, Martin.' Liv could feel Ryan's eyes burning over her and she was forced to stop as he stood solidly blocking their exit. As he was looking straight at her she felt obliged to make some explanations. 'I've decided I'll go home now, Ryan. I have a headache. Martin has kindly offered me a lift as Joel is taking your father home.'

'Yes, I know he is. I've been talking to him outside.' His eyes went to Martin. 'If you'll wait a moment I'll take you home.'

'No, no, you can't leave your guests,' Liv tried to smile, 'and Martin doesn't mind, do you, Martin?'

'Of course not. Well, you'll excuse us, Denison?' Martin moved forward and for a moment Liv thought Ryan was going to continue blocking the doorway, but he stepped aside, his face set.

'A successful evening,' Martin remarked. 'No doubt you're pleased.' His tone even set Liv's teeth on edge.

'Yes, quite pleased,' answered Ryan, his mouth tight and his eyes moved back to Liv. 'I'll see you, Liv,' he said ominously, and she shivered as she walked past him almost feeling his anger reach out and touch her.

'I'm sorry I made an exhibition of myself earlier, Olivia,' said Martin as they drove around the bay. 'I really can't understand what came over me. I do hope you'll forgive me.'

Liv sighed, wishing Martin would increase the

speed of the car. She wanted to be home and alone and Martin's sedate crawl was playing on her nerves. 'I've forgotten about it already.'

'That's very generous of you, Olivia. I would like to say that I deeply regret the disruption of our friendship.'

Liv looked up from studying her hands in her lap, straining through the darkness. Yes, there was the bungalow. She almost sighed with relief. 'Thank you, Martin. It was all my fault. I'm afraid I didn't want to discuss my marriage with anyone.'

'That's not hard to understand,' Martin said generously. 'I believe he arrived unexpectedly?'

'Yes, quite unexpectedly.' Liv swung the passenger door open before Martin had a chance to switch off the ignition. 'Thank you for dropping me home. I do appreciate it.' She stepped quickly from the car.

'My pleasure, Olivia.' He paused, trying to decide whether or not to invite himself inside. 'Well, I'll say goodnight. Take a couple of aspirins for that headache.'

Liv almost ran inside and leaned weakly back against the front door expelling a long breath of release. She had been prepared for Martin to expect a cup of coffee and she wanted to avoid that at all costs. She couldn't have borne his questions or his sanctimonious advice.

In her room she wearily kicked off her shoes and sank on to the chair in front of her dressing table, picking up her cream for removing her make-up. She felt she moved with an exaggeratedly slow motion and her face was pale, her eyes large and over-bright.

Lethargically she turned down her bed and her

head throbbed painfully. What she needed was a nice hot cup of tea, and if she forced herself she could summon the energy to make it. She splashed her face with cool water before walking into the kitchen and setting the water to boil, refusing to allow her troubled mind to dwell on the evening or on Ryan's cold face as she left him.

Carrying the steaming cup of tea into the living room, she subsided into her favourite chair and sipped the hot soothing liquid. She supposed she should go to bed, Maria could be returning the children fairly early, but standing up, undressing, showering, demanded an effort and she rested her head back and closed her eyes.

The restrained slam of a car door brought her eyes open again and she almost hoped it was Martin returning, all the while knowing before she reached the window that the silver Mercedes would be there, gleaming mockingly in the moonlight. She had known from the moment she had left him that he would follow her.

But when the knock came on the door she stood transfixed, not making a sound. The doorknob rattled and the knocking became louder.

'Liv, open up!' His voice held so much command that she found herself in the hallway before she realised she had moved.

'Liv, open the door or I swear I'll bust it in!'

'Ryan, it's late. I was about to go to bed——' Liv's voice trembled.

'Liv!' The word was constrainedly quiet and she reluctantly unlocked the door.

He was leaning with one hand against the door

jamb and he had shed his jacket and tie, leaving his shirt partially unbuttoned, and his hair fell forward in disorder.

He straightened and Liv stood aside for him to enter before she closed the door and followed him into the living room. Wishing she had the added advantage of height that her shoes would have given her, she decided to take the offensive, let him see she wasn't to be intimidated.

'Would you mind saying what you have to say and then going. I'm tired and I'm in no mood to swap insults with you.'

He smiled crookedly, his hands on his hips, his shirt straining across his chest. 'I'll say this for you, Liv, you've got spirit, and that didn't show eight years ago.'

'Perhaps you didn't look for it?'

'Maybe. Maybe not.' He regarded her through narrowed eyes. 'I half expected to find Wilson still here. Or has he been and gone?' His tone put a different connotation on the innocent words.

Liv quelled a spurt of anger with no little difficulty. 'Martin drove me home and then left. He knew I was tired,' she said pointedly.

'I guess he's on cloud nine now that he's got a foot back in the door.'

'And just what is that supposed to mean?' she asked tersely.

Shrugging arrogantly, he turned and prowled over to the window. 'Stop kidding yourself about that stuffed shirt. I know you, Liv, and he's not for you. Never in a million years.'

'Is that a studied observation or simply your bruised

ego talking?' she asked disdainfully.

His head went up as he spun back to face her, his eyes glittering dangerously before narrowing to mere slits.

Liv's heart fluttered in fright. She was mesmerised like a small animal cornered by a predator, and she could feel the pulse at the base of her throat beating agitatedly.

He shoved his hands into his pockets with some force, as though he didn't trust himself were they left unrestrained. 'Are you really as brave as your words, Mrs Denison? I wonder.'

'It's rather petty of you to criticise Martin. He's reliable, considerate and a stable person.' Liv wondered if the words sounded as hollow to him as they did to her own ears.

A mocking smile lifted one corner of his mouth. 'All that I'm not, in other words?' The smile left his face. 'But tell me this, Liv. Does he strike as big a spark with you as I do? I mean, we only have to look at each other and it bursts into a thousand flames. Deny that if you can. That's how it's always been with us and always will be. If I touched you now I'd see the truth in your eyes, wouldn't I?'

Liv took a step backwards and that same cynical smile brushed his mouth and died away. 'Have you been to bed with him yet?'

'No, I . . .' Liv's face flamed at the shock his blatant words gave her. 'Why, you . . .' she gulped a breath. 'If I have it's no business of yours. If I chose to take on an entire football team I wouldn't ask your permission!'

As soon as the words were out she felt the horror

spread over her, leaving a bitter taste in her mouth, making her feel unclean and humiliated. She couldn't even feel fear as she watched Ryan's face turn pale with anger as he took one threatening step towards her before he stopped, running a distracted hand through his hair.

'What is it you want, Liv?' he asked angrily. 'Passionate entreaties of undying love? Flowery phrases to please your romantic heart? Well, that's not my scene. I'm not a word man, it's actions with me. And maybe that's what you want, too.'

'Oh, you're so good at that, aren't you?' Liv cried, throwing discretion to the wind. 'That's what it's all about as far as you're concerned. Actions. Take what you want. Well, there's more to it than just the physical side, Ryan. A relationship needs more than sex to keep it alive. And if the bedroom's all you've got on your mind then I'm sorry for you.'

'Oh, that's on my mind, believe me,' he said with feeling. 'Whenever you're around it doesn't leave my mind.' He reached her in one stride, his hands biting into the flesh of her arms, dragging her against him.

'Ryan! Leave me alone!' She turned her head aside from his seeking lips. 'You're driving me insane!'

'And what do you think you're doing to me, every waking moment of the day? And at night, it's worse. You haunt my dreams.' His hand gripped her jaw, turning her face so that he could look into her frightened eyes. 'You're like a virus I've contracted, Liv. Just when I think I've got you out of my system you recur to strike me down again.'

His hand moved around beneath her hair to cup the back of her head, his thumb tracing her jawline, her cheek, her earlobe. Her eyes were fixed on the sensual curve of his lips.

'God, you're more beautiful, more . . . Liv . . .' His mouth descended on hers with a hunger he seemed powerless to control.

His arms crushed her to him, moulding her to the hard contours of his body. Her struggles made little or no impression on him and she could feel the response he was demanding beginning to rise within her. His hands found the zipper at her back and the black dress slid to the floor, left to fall in disarray, with total disregard or respect for its exclusiveness or expense.

'Ryan, please! Stop this now,' Liv made an effort to fight the passion he had kindled and fanned into a raging fire, rising to consume her, 'before I have more reason to despise you!'

'You know something?' he laughed harshly, self-derisively. 'You're going to have to stand in line because I despise myself. But neither can I help myself.' His hands moved over her almost desperately and his lips plundered the softness of her neck. 'I couldn't stop now if the sky fell in,' he murmured thickly, lifting her into his arms as though she was a feather-weight and carrying her into the bedroom.

He deposited her on the bed she had so recently turned down and she lay and watched him. She knew she should have made an effort to get out while he pulled off his shirt, stepped out of his slacks, but she lay and watched him, enmeshed, captured by the burning fire in those blue eyes now black as coal, impaling her.

His hard body moved over hers and then she was lost. And soon she had no desire to escape him at all.

It was as he had said it was, and she burned for him with a fire that matched his own. This night, and that night on the beach all those years ago, became the only reality, and their union was as right as it had been before the outside world had stumbled upon them and their bubble had burst.

CHAPTER TEN

LIV stirred, trying to stretch her aching muscles, her body sending signals to her brain, telling her she was restricted, pinned beneath an unaccustomed weight, and in her semi-wakefulness she moved agitatedly, coming fully alert to stare at the tanned shoulder that lay so close beside her in the narrow bed. Her eyes rose to the dark head and met his slightly guarded blue eyes. For immeasurable moments they stared at each other and a bright blush rose to her cheeks as recollections of the night before surged into her mind. Was it only a few hours ago that they had been lost in each other, oblivious to all else save their lovemaking?

She cringed at her own weakness. How could she have let it happen? she taunted herself, and when Ryan went to draw her into his arms she sprang off the bed and struggled into her terry towelling bathrobe, knotting the belt tightly about her waist.

Ryan lay on the bed, all solid muscle, making no attempt to draw the covers over himself.

'I think you'd better go, Ryan,' she said, turning

her eyes away from that body even now evoking memories which made her shiver inside. She could almost feel the remembered hardness of him plundering her softness.

'What? No breakfast?' he asked drily. 'Even a condemned man gets a meal.'

'I just want you to get dressed and go.' Liv's voice rose higher and she took a deep steadying breath, pulling herself back from the verge of hysteria. 'I never want to see you again!' She moved farther away from him.

'Oh? You never want to see me again?' he repeated levelly, his voice as low and controlled as hers had been high and distraught. 'Because I made love to you, I suppose?'

'Made love? Is that what you call it?' she threw back at him.

'Whatever you want to call it, it was a mutual thing. I didn't have to do much convincing. Be honest with yourself, Liv—you wanted me as much as I wanted you. So what's this outraged, hypocritical act in aid of?' he asked brutally.

'You're hateful!' she cried. 'And for God's sake, get dressed!'

He stood looking at her disdainfully before slowly picking up his clothes and climbing into them. 'You didn't object to our déshabille last night, Mrs Denison.'

'Will you shut up about last night! I don't want to hear any more about it.' Liv put her hands over her ears, biting back the urge to scream at him.

He walked across the room to her, his shirt unbuttoned, and pulled her hands down to her sides, holding them there in an inflexible grip. 'You are one hell of a bitch, Liv.' His eyes raked her figure, settling on the belt of her robe, and for a moment she thought he would wrench it undone, but he smiled with mocking coldness. 'There isn't a piece of cloth in Australia that could keep me from touching you if I wanted you,' he said arrogantly. 'So stop this childishness and let's behave like rational adults.' He let her go and raked a hand through his hair.

'You think you're so irresistible, don't you? The great Ryan Denison! Everyone has to fall in with what you want.'

'We both want the same thing,' he said, and pulled her into his arms, his lips moving over hers arousingly.

When her lips began a trembling response she shoved against him. Ryan released her and his knowing smile was the last straw. Her hand snaked up and stung his cheek, the sound echoing about the bedroom.

His jaw set tightly, the imprint of her hand clearly visible on his face. 'I should give you a hiding for that, but I'm beginning to think you're not worth the effort.' He spun on his heel, sending the bedroom door back against the wall with a crash that rattled the cosmetic bottles on Liv's dressing table. 'You can find me at the yacht when you've come to your senses.'

'You'll have a long wait, Ryan, because if I never see you again it will be too soon!' Her voice rose as she followed him into the hallway.

'Perhaps you're right at that,' he said harshly as he opened the front door. 'It's time I put this place behind me once and for all—and don't expect me back.'

They both stopped when they saw the twins standing on the steps, their young faces stricken as Maria hurried along the path, obviously coming to see what the trouble was. That the twins had heard their raised voices Liv could see in their horrified eyes.

'I'll see you, kids.' Ryan's voice was a little quieter and he strode past them and was roaring away with a spinning of wheels in the loose gravel before any of them could make a move.

Melly's sobs brought Liv back to earth as the little girl wrapped her arms around Liv's waist, pressing her face against her mother.

'Liv, I'm sorry,' Maria began, her face full of concern, 'they were out of the car before I knew . . . before I could stop them.'

'It's not your fault, Maria. We . . . I didn't realise it was so late.' Liv held Melly closely. 'Don't cry, love. There's nothing to cry about. It's all right.'

'Why were you and Daddy yelling like that? Luke and I thought you liked each other and that we'd all be together like a real family,' Melly gulped.

Filled with compassion, Maria's eyes met Liv's.

'Look, Melly. Sometimes adults disagree and they argue, just the way you and Luke often have little disagreements.'

'But, Mummy, you looked so angry, and I don't think Daddy will be coming back,' she sobbed.

'Oh, Melly! Just because Daddy and I have an argument it doesn't mean he's angry with you and Luke,' Liv assured them both.

'But we don't want him to be angry with you either.' Melly's voice caught on a sob.

'Come on, now, no more tears. How about thanking Aunt Maria for taking care of you last night?' Liv tried to put as much cheerfulness into her voice as she could.

'Thank you, Aunt Maria,' they chorused, although Melly still clung to Liv and Luke's troubled gaze rested on his mother.

'Thanks from me, too, Maria,' Liv said brightly. 'It was a successful evening for Ryan.' She almost stumbled over the words.

'That's good. Well, I'll get back if you're sure you're all right. Mike has a short shift today, so we can have a nice family dinner for a change.'

Over breakfast the twins sat morosely pushing their cornflakes about their bowls and, unable to stand the quietness any longer, Liv set her spoon down and looked levelly at them both.

'Luke—Melly—I'm sorry you had to overhear our argument this morning and I want you to try not to let it worry you. You both know that your father and I haven't seen each other for a long time and it takes some time to get to know each other again. Sometimes you find you don't agree about a lot of things.'

The twins looked solemnly back at her.

'But our argument had nothing to do with you two and it doesn't make any difference to the fact that we love you both very much.'

'But you don't love each other, is that it?' asked Luke flatly.

'Perhaps we don't love each other in quite the same way.' Liv's heart felt bruised.

'Won't Daddy be coming to live with us, then?' asked Melly, her lip trembling.

'How can he come and live with us if he's going away?' Luke frowned at his sister and a tear trickled down her cheek. 'I guess there'll just be the three of us, like before?' he sighed.

'I guess so,' said Liv, wishing she could allow her tears to fall like Melly was doing.

Liv stirred awake, looking around for the twins. They had been playing on the beach while she sat on the patio and her draining evening had caught up with her and she had dozed off.

'Melly? Luke?' she called into the quietness. There was no answer. She glanced at her watch and started in surprise. Surely she couldn't have been asleep for an hour and a half? Walking down into the garden, she called a little louder.

Five minutes later she knew there was no sign of them inside or around the house. Her gaze went to the water so close by and her heart almost stopped beating in terror. No! No, they never went into the water alone. That was a rule she enforced with no exceptions. But where would they have gone? She strained her eyes, scanning both ends of the bay, but the beach was deserted.

Maybe they were riding their bicycles. She flew around to the garage and saw that their bicycles had indeed gone. However, her momentary relief was followed by fear again. They never went anywhere without telling her. Perhaps they hadn't wanted to wake her. Her eyes now searched the road, but that was empty, too.

Forcing calmness, she tried to decide where they could have gone. The Costellos'—that was the most logical place. Running inside, she dialled the number, letting it ring for some time before acknowledging that no one was home.

Twenty minutes later Liv was almost frantic. She had rung all of their friends that she could recall and drawn a complete blank. No one had seen them.

Joel. Of course! That was where they'd be. She picked up the phone again. She would read them both the riot act when she got hold of them!

'Denison residence.'

'Oh, Thomas, this is Liv. Is Joel there?'

'No, Miss Liv, no one's home. Mr Joel took Mr Denison and Mr Mallory on a drive about the area. They left nearly two hours ago.'

'Oh!' Liv's heart sank again. 'You haven't seen the twins, have you?'

'No, Miss Liv, they're not here.'

Liv dropped the receiver and almost gave way to panic. What should she do? Who could she . . .? Ryan. She'd ring him. If he hadn't left already. She was oblivious of the tears falling down her cheeks as she dialled the number of the caretaker of the wharf.

'Jim? This is Liv Denison. Is Ryan's yacht still anchored in the bay?' she asked breathlessly.

'It's in at the wharf here, Liv. He brought her in this morning.'

'Do you know if Ryan's on board?' she prayed silently.

'He was earlier on, but he came ashore after lunch and drove off towards Airlie. Can I give him a message when I see him?'

'Oh. Oh, no, Jim, it doesn't matter.' Liv covered her face with her hands. She had to do something. She'd have to get in her car and drive around looking for them. Her imagination painted colourful pictures of what could have happened to them and she ran out of the front door as though her feet had wings. At the sight of Ryan climbing from the Mercedes Liv's control snapped completely and she flew into his arms on the verge of hysteria.

'Liv, calm down! Calm down and tell me what's wrong.' He shook her firmly.

'I can't find the twins. They've gone,' she said through chattering teeth. 'I've called everyone I can think of and no one's seen them. Oh, Ryan, where can they be?'

'Now, take a hold of yourself. Come inside and we'll work from there.' His calmness steadied her a little. 'Mike and Maria haven't seen them?'

She shook her head. 'I rang them first, but they weren't home.'

'What's their number? I'll try again.'

But there was still no answer and he replaced the receiver. No sooner had he done this than the phone pealed and Liv jumped to her feet, her face pale.

'Ryan Denison here.'

'Jim Ferguson down at the wharf. Glad I caught you, Ryan. Look, one of the boys said he saw two nippers on your boat a few minutes ago and I found two bicycles behind my shed belonging to the twins. I thought I'd check to see if they're supposed to be there or not.'

'Thanks for ringing, Jim. We'll come down right away. Keep your eye on the boat, will you, until we get there?'

'Sure thing, Ryan.'

'Has he found them? Are they all right?'

'They're on the boat.'

'On the boat? Oh, Ryan!' Liv sagged and he grabbed her shoulders. 'Are they alone?'

'So it appears. Do you feel up to coming with me?' He let her stand by herself, dropping his hands to his sides.

'Yes. Yes, I'm all right.'

'Right, let's go.'

There was no sign of life on the yacht, but Jim assured them that no one had left since he phoned. Ryan helped Liv jump on board and he scanned the upper deck. 'Luke? Melly?'

There was no answer and fear clutched at Liv again.

'I'll look below.' Ryan went down into the main cabin with Liv close on his heels. 'Wait here.' He searched the forward cabin and returned, shaking his head as he passed her to go into the stern section. He was longer this time and finally reappeared with the twins held firmly by their arms.

'Thank God!' Liv sank down and drew them both to her. 'Oh, Luke, Melly—I've been nearly out of my mind with worry!' Tears of relief ran down her face and both children burst into distressed sobbing.

'We were scared, Mummy,' wept Melly. 'We thought Daddy would come back, but he didn't, so we hid inside.'

'Why didn't you tell your mother you were coming down here, Luke?' Ryan asked gently but firmly.

'Mum was asleep,' he said chokedly, looking ashamedly at the floor, 'and we—well, we thought if we ran away and hid on your boat and you sailed away when you found us you'd have to bring us back

to Mum and then you wouldn't go away again.'
Luke's voice broke and Ryan put his arms around
him, holding him close until his sobs abated. 'We
didn't mean to make you scared, Mum.'

Walking into the bathroom Ryan returned with a
hand towel. 'Is this big enough to dry all these tears?'
he asked, and Melly gave a halfhearted giggle as he
mopped firstly her face and then Luke's. 'How about
Mummy?' he asked, and putting one hand behind
Liv's head he gently wiped her eyes, letting the soft
towel move down over her damp cheek and across her
lips.

Their eyes met and he was looking at her in such a
way that Liv's knees very nearly gave way beneath
her and her heart skipped erratically. His hand drew
her head against his shoulder and he held her tightly
for a moment before standing back.

'I'll bet you've worked up an appetite,' he turned
to the twins. 'Shall we eat here or go home?'

'If we go home will you come, too?' asked Melly.

Neither Liv nor Ryan spoke.

'Will you?' asked Luke.

Ryan's eyes lifted to Liv with that same devastating wanting in their blue depths. 'Will I, Liv?' he
asked huskily, a note in his voice she hadn't heard
before.

'We'd like you to,' she said at last, and it was as
though a final weight was lifted from her heart and
the bitterness of the years between crumbled away.

It wasn't until much later when the twins were
finally tucked into bed and Liv was making a cup of
coffee that the realisation that they were alone at last
hit her. They had a lot of talking to do and now that

the time had come Liv was loath to begin. She cast a quick glance at him through her lashes to find him watching her.

'I didn't ask how you came to return this afternoon?' she said to cover her flush of embarrassment.

He smiled. 'The excuse I was going to use escaped me the moment you threw yourself into my arms. I thought all my Christmases had come at once.'

She laughed breathlessly. 'Ryan, be serious!'

'Oh, I assure you, I am serious. I've never been more serious in my life.'

He moved across to stand close beside her and she handed him his coffee while her heart thudded deafeningly in her ears. Setting his cup back on the bench, he pulled her into his arms, resting his cheek against her temple.

'Nothing means a thing to me without you,' he said simply, and leant back to look down into her eyes and smiled ruefully. 'Last night when I decried flowery speeches—well, now I'm hoist with my own petard, because that's just what I want to do. Only I can't seem to find the words. All I can say is that I love you—I always have, I always will.'

'Oh, Ryan! I love you, too.' Tears glistened on her lashes as she slid her arms around his waist and leant weakly against him.

They stood together for some time and then Ryan led her outside on to the patio, and sitting in an easy chair, he pulled her on to his knee and sighed appreciatively.

'You've led me one hell of a dance, Mrs Denison. I hope you're suitably ashamed of yourself,' he grinned.

'I led you?' Liv chided him gently. 'You've had me on a string since I was six years old!'

He chuckled. 'You've hidden that fact very well these past few weeks. It was only when I kissed you that I took any heart,' he told her, and proceeded to put his statement to the test, very thoroughly. The kiss deepened and they were both breathless when they drew apart.

'Was I so transparent?' Liv laughed shakily.

'Not in the least,' he said with feeling. 'I was even dead green with jealousy when you looked at Joel.' His eyes probed her face. 'But I can be sure now, can't I?'

Liv nodded and he held her against him tightly.

'I came back this afternoon to ask you to come with me when I left,' he said quietly, 'if you wanted to leave, if there were too many unhappy memories around here. After last night I . . .' he took a deep breath, 'I've spent all day calling myself all kinds of a fool. Selfish, thoughtless, weak—you name it. Liv, I couldn't leave you and the kids behind me again. It was bad enough in the beginning. But now, it would have been impossible for me to have gone and kept my sanity. This afternoon I was going to beg you to let me stay.' He finished on a note of remembered agony.

'You wouldn't have needed to do that,' she told him. 'Oh, Ryan, I was so utterly despondent when you left. I guess as the years went by I allowed myself to grow bitter. Then you turned up without warning and turned my world upside down. I realised I was as attracted to you as I ever was and I was afraid I'd get hurt again. I couldn't face going through the anguish of those first few months once more.'

Ryan closed his eyes. 'If only you knew how much I wanted to take you with me! Why do you think I left without seeing you after the wedding? Because I knew I wouldn't have had the strength to leave you behind if I'd seen you again—and that's the truth.' Some of the torment was there on his face.

'But why didn't you ask me to go with you? You must have known I was crazy about you.'

'I thought you were too young and that you simply had a teenage crush on me, and it wasn't hard for D.J. and your father to convince me I was right about that. I already despised myself for losing my self-control and causing you the humiliation of that night. They didn't have any trouble persuading me I was irresponsible and that it would be best if I left you to pick up the threads of your life without me. I half believed it before they started.'

'Oh, Ryan, I wish someone had asked me what I wanted. Where did you go? No one ever mentioned you to me.'

'Just about everywhere. I'm not proud of those first two years. I was bitter and I believed I was all the things our fathers called me, and I'm afraid I acted accordingly, living hard, playing hard. I did a good job of being decadent. Drinking, gambling—you name it. And I tried my level best to forget you, too, but that was an impossibility. I had you in my blood, in every living breath I took.' His hand moved gently on her arm.

'All my money slipped through my fingers and then I had one stroke of luck. I won a stack of money in a poker game. How I did it I don't know to this day.

I was pretty drunk at the time and while I was making my way back to my hotel some of the losers tried to get even with me. That's where I met Kim Sukuna. He happened to be passing the alley with Roko and they came to my aid, saved my skin and the money.'

Liv was horrified. 'Were you hurt?'

'No more than I deserved to be,' he said self-derogatorily. 'I spent some time talking to Kim and then I decided to come home.'

'You came back here? But . . . no one told me,' Liv looked at him in surprise. 'You didn't come to see me,' she said flatly.

'You were the reason I did come back,' he said definitely. 'I came to take you with me, to share my exile.' He laughed mirthlessly and shook his head. 'But fortunately the first person I met when I arrived from the airport was Joel. And my first shock was reading the horror in his eyes. I must have been a degrading sight—rumpled suit, unshaven, long hair. Before I knew where I was he'd whisked me away and cleaned me up.'

'Joel should have told me,' Liv began, but Ryan put a finger to her lips.

'No, Liv, he shouldn't have. You don't know how bad a state I was in. We talked, and he gave me a tongue-lashing that would have done D.J. proud. He really pulled out the stops, and with good reason. At one stage he threatened to tie me up and toss me in the harbour before he'd let me get near you as I was then.'

'I just can't believe it.' Liv shook her head. 'Joel never once let anything slip. I suppose it was Joel who told you about the twins?'

Ryan looked a little sheepish. 'Do you remember the couple of afternoons you left the twins with Joel while you visited Maria when she was in hospital with appendicitis?'

Liv nodded.

'Joel asked me over and presented me with the twins in person. I was staggered. If anything sobered me up once and for all, that did. I watched you arriving and leaving the house and—well, I left my heart here with you.' He paused. 'They're beaut kids, Liv,' he said huskily.

'I know,' she laughed shakily. 'Do you suppose we could try for triplets next time?'

'That sounds remarkably like a proposition, Mrs Denison,' Ryan chuckled.

'It is, Mr Denison.' Liv's arms went around his neck.

'Oh, Liv! If you look at me like that I'll never get to tell you all that needs to be said.' He crushed her to him before continuing. 'Seeing the twins finally convinced me. I knew I had to go and not come back until I had myself together. I felt such a heel.' He ran a gentle finger down her cheek. 'Can you forgive me for putting you through all that? Leaving you to face it alone?'

'I never once regretted having the twins or marrying you. All I ever wanted was to be with you, and having the twins—well, it was my compensation.' She saw the pain in his eyes.

'Joel told me how upset you were when I left and I didn't want to rake it up again for you, so I left as suddenly as I arrived, and from that moment I made myself a promise. I remembered Craven Island, all my old ideas for it, and I've worked towards that these past six years. I was beginning to think I'd taken too long,' he finished softly.

'I've been so miserable, thinking you'd bought the island to get back at D.J. and imagining you wanted us back to clinch the deal with Mrs Craven.' Liv sighed. 'I was so afraid to let myself trust you, and my fear turned to anger, directed mostly at myself. I . . . I wanted you to suffer some of the anguish I did without you, thinking you didn't care. My pride rose and stopped me doing what I desperately wanted to do.'

'And what was that?' A small smile played around the corners of his mouth as he settled her more comfortably on his lap.

'To fall into your arms.'

'What a coincidence,' he chuckled. 'I desperately wanted the chance to catch you, too.' He touched a kiss to the tip of her nose. 'That block of land up on the hill that I bought from Mrs Craven—would you like to live there? I hoped we could design and build our home together, up there overlooking the Whitsundays. What do you say?'

'I say anywhere as long as I'm with you,' she said truthfully.

'Those words are music to my ears, my love.' The expression in his eyes belied the humour of his words and he lifted her hand, touching his lips softly to her palm. 'Now I've got you in my arms, Liv, I'll never let you go again.' His lips claimed hers and they clung together ardently, each knowing how close they had come to losing each other.

Ryan took a deep steadying breath. 'Are you going to send me home tonight?' he asked, his eyes ignited by the flame of their spiralling senses. 'I mean, do you suppose Melly would be outraged to find me in your bed in the morning?'

'There's a divan in my studio,' she told him, a smile teasing the corners of her mouth, 'you could sleep there.'

'Could I now?' He nuzzled her earlobe. 'You're a hard woman, Liv Denison. But I think I'm going to enjoy talking you into sharing that divan with me,' he said, and proceeded to do just that.

Masquerade
Historical Romances

Intrigue excitement romance

DAUGHTER OF ISIS
by *Belinda Grey*

A few weeks ago she had been Ellen Parry of Cwm Bedd in Wales, never likely to travel very much further afield. Now she was in the land of the pyramids, and a mysterious man on a white horse seemed determined to block her every move . . .

STRANGER IN THE GLEN
by *Isobel Stewart*

When her parents died, Rosemary Lockhart made her home with her mother's old friend, Elspeth Macrae of Glen Ardrachan. But when Elspeth's Jacobite son returned home, he made it clear that *he* had no welcome for a stranger — particularly an English girl!

Look out for these titles in your local paperback shop from
12th June 1981

Doctor Nurse Romances

and June's
stories of romantic relationships behind the scenes
of modern medical life are:

NURSE AT SEA
by Judith Worthy

Nurse Carole Wilson hopes a long sea voyage from
Australia to Britain will solve her emotional problems.
But when she finds the Ship's Surgeon is an old
boyfriend of hers, it is a case of out of the frying
pan into the fire . . .

THE UNWILLING LOVE
by Lucy Bowdler

Janice Colby starts her first job at Nootak — as nurse
to Eskimos — and has a warm welcome from everyone
except the handsome Mountie Philip Anson, who is as
chilly as the surroundings.

Order your copies today from your local paperback retailer.